MW01643921

The Legend

A tale of eternal possibility

Bonny Gilbert Ashe

This is a work of fiction. Names, characters, places, and incidents either are the product of the author's imagination or are used fictitiously. Any resemblance to actual events or locales or persons, living or dead, is entirely coincidental.

ISBN 0-7414-5654-0

Published by:

1094 New DeHaven Street, Suite 100
West Conshohocken, PA 19428-2713
Info@buybooksontheweb.com
www.buybooksontheweb.com
Toll-free (877) BUY BOOK
Local Phone (610) 941-9999
Fax (610) 941-9959

Printed in the United States of America

Published October 2009

Acknowledgement and Dedication

A friend once told me that humans are incapable of imagining anything they cannot create. With those words, I disposed of all the early warnings I had been given about "not letting my imagination run away with me." This book is dedicated to the possibility thinkers in my life, and they include family members, teachers and friends, and four wonderful Maine Coon cats who kept me company during the hours of musing and writing. A special thanks to Rev. Richard Rogers, whose challenge to "write a legend" jump started this project, and to Anita Gilbert for her illustrations. More than anyone else, I am grateful to my husband Christopher, who actually believes I can do anything.

Bonny Gilbert Ashe

September, 2009

Table of Contents

Prologue

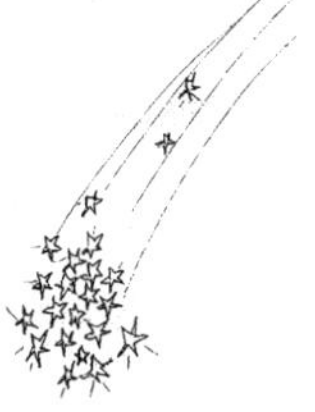

So great has been the endurance, so incredible the achievement, that, as long as the sun keeps a set course in heaven, it would be foolish to despair of the human race.

Ernest L. Woodward

She peered out the window, watching her great grandchildren come toward her house. They paused often to pet a dog, pick a flower, hopscotch over cracks in the sidewalk and run sticks along a picket fence. They were always excited to visit Nanna's house but, as children do, they were captured in the moment by one delight after another. The brother and sister were just a year apart in age and completely entranced with each other. She watched them coming, knowing the afternoon with them would tire her yet treasuring every bit of it. She would be moving soon to an assisted living facility and wouldn't see them as often. It was too far away for them to walk and their busy parents would make excuses and apologies for not bringing them more frequently. But she had today with them, and a few more like it. They unfailingly made her laugh. Their questions caused her to think more deeply than she had in her whole life. Both of them thought her beautiful, in spite of her age. What better companions could you hope for? They would be memories she would hold like a precious treasure.

Nanna! The two of them burst through the door in a happy tumble of giggles and fingerprints. "We're thirsty! Do you have cookies?" She smiled at them fondly. "Go wash your hands; heaven knows what you've been touching, then meet me on the back porch." They were back in minutes, half washed and half dried hands dripping as they came. They dove for the apple juice, nabbed a couple of cookies and settled in the porch swing with great anticipation. "Nanna, you promised to tell us the story of the great war between light and darkness and the heroes who won it. Please, will you tell us now?"

"It was not a war," Nanna insisted. "Don't even use that word. The idea of war must die completely in human minds if life on this earth is going to be good for everyone. There was a great struggle and it brought about the peace we have enjoyed for three generations now. There is nothing wrong with struggle. It hones you and makes everyone stronger, but in war some must lose and that makes everyone weaker, even the apparent winners. Now, I have decided that since you two think this was a war, I must tell you the whole story from the beginning, so you will understand what really happened. That means we won't finish it today. You must come back next time and next to hear the whole tale." The children's eyes lit up at the idea of extended story times with Nanna. She could tell a tale like no one else.

Great grandmother took a deep breath, and looking fondly at the children, bathed their surroundings in a golden glow of love before beginning her tale. "The story begins with the birth of a baby girl, and winds through many places and times", she said. "But I promise, every word is true."

In the Beginning

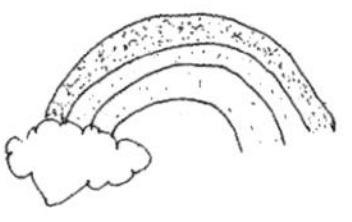

"Lots of people talk to animals," said Pooh.
"Maybe, but..."
"Not very many listen, though," he said.
"That's the problem," he added.

Winnie the Pooh A. A. Milne

At 6:36 AM she emerged into a cold room with white tile walls, harsh lights and many hard surfaces. In spite of the discomfort, it was a relief to partially separate from the intense fear of the one who brought her here. She vaguely remembered willingly leaving the warm comfort of Mother to come to this place. She and Mother were so excited at the shining brilliance of the Spirit Journey she was launching. They dreamed places and times she would cross, and set opportunities and choices in motion for what she would encounter in these places and times. They wrote reminders of all this in patterns she could recognize as she traveled her Spirit Journey.

There would be wonderful companions who remembered Mother as well, and they could all speak with each other in a way most could not understand. Best of all, each of them would be bringing a purpose to the places they would inhabit. Each of them would have their own purpose, and, as they lived it, they would be filled with joy. Their joy would be an attracting force for others, and marvelous things would happen when these others each learned to discover and live their own purpose. "What was that now?" She strained to capture a fleeting idea but it eluded her. Mother promised she would remember when the time was ripe, but she never dreamed she would begin to forget so quickly.

Right now she was in a whirl of confusion. The sounds and smells and the chill in the air were alien and frightening. How did she get here? She remembered she had just spent a long time growing a body under a nervous and often pounding heart. This heart really wanted a child and she was becoming a child, so she told herself "it would surely be OK. Of course this world would love her and nurture her journey, wouldn't it? She and Mother had talked about it. Hadn't they?"

But when she emerged into this cold and noisy place she lost her guidance systems. She had little control of this new body she had worked so long to make. She willed herself to the other side of the room, but nothing happened. She roared a message to those around her, but she could tell no one heard. She was trapped and immobilized, arms waving and legs kicking helplessly.

She could feel the other beings around her. A couple of them were delighted and fulfilled by her successful birth. Their lights were shining very brightly. One had been up all night and just wanted food and sleep. That one's light was gentle but fuzzy. Another was bored and disinterested. "My tenth baby this week. There has to be something fun to do. I need a break." That light was jittery and funny colored.

Then there was the biggest one. Waves of power rippled from her form, but the very center of her essence was a black, bottomless hole. She pressed her thumb firmly in the center of the girl-child's forehead and a roar waved out of her. "NO! You may not do that here." The thumb pressed harder between the baby girl's eyes. "NO! What you bring is forbidden. Abandon it or die!"

The room had gotten very quiet. A heavy pall in the air made it hard to breathe and no one seemed to be moving. A faint, golden glow slipped into the room and surrounded the infant. Then the biggest one slipped away and the rest seemed to come awake with a start, then go about their work as though they had noticed nothing unusual. The newborn lustily screamed her displeasure, which appeared to please everyone else.

She was wrapped in something warm and soft then carried to the woman who had helped her grow a body. The woman's fear had dissolved and little flashes of joy were coming from her heart. Her mate leaned over and kissed them both. "The doctor said she is healthy," the woman said. "She won't die like our first daughter. We're a family now."

The baby didn't understand the words, but she could feel the relief and happiness coming from the pair. Perhaps this Spirit Journey would be good after all. It troubled her that she couldn't quite remember what it was – something to do with light and darkness - and the thought of the thumb of the dark one sent a shiver through her. But right now she was being offered food so she settled contentedly in the warm arms of the woman.

The pair made a fuss over her, noticing her hair would be very dark and wondering what color her eyes would be. The woman's eyes were green, and the man's were deep brown; nearly black. She was a bit startled when they named her Beauty. Mother had said, "A name is supposed to remind you of what you promised your life would be." "What does Beauty have to do with my Spirit Journey?"

she thought, as she drifted off to sleep. The images of her new home filled her awareness, leaving no room to dream of Mother or where she had lived before starting this new body. She dreamed of bright lights surrounding her, and a dark, heavy cloud hiding in a corner not far away.

After a few days, the pair carried her to their own home where it was warm and welcoming, and the dreams of the dark one disappeared. Other family members visited, bringing gifts, and there was so much joy. These people had such hopes for the life she would live. She could see the pictures in their minds, and they made her a bit nervous even though they were filled with love and optimism. In one dream she was wearing rich, heavy clothing, and in another, standing in a marble hall. A third dream showed her kneeling alone in a tiny room, her hair covered and her head bowed. She didn't understand any of them, and somehow seeing the dream-pictures made her lose more of the memory of her Spirit Journey. She fussed fitfully at that, and someone decided she needed her diaper changed.

Sometimes when she was alone, a shining one came to visit her. They talked without speaking and Beauty always felt happier and safer when they were together. She didn't know the name of the shining one, or even if it was a male or a female, or if that even mattered in this strange new place. When she asked, "Who are you?" the visitor smiled and let her know she would remember one day. Meanwhile it promised to always help her be safe. The shining one seemed to be the only one who understood speaking without words. She learned to call this kind of speaking her 'secret voice.'

In time the girl learned the people language. She could ask for what she wanted and make them smile with a soft "I love you" and make them laugh when she sang and danced. She learned the pair who raised her were her

Mommy and Daddy, and there were grandmas and aunts and uncles. Then one day Daddy went away on a big ship for a long time, and everyone was always delighted when she sang "Bell bottom trousers, coat of navy blue. I love my daddy and he loves me too." Sometimes she would sing the song on a bus when a favorite aunt took her shopping, and often someone would give her a nickel after clapping their approval.

Beauty and Mommy lived with Grandma Mary while Daddy was away on the big ship. She was told Grandpa had died, but she didn't know what that meant. She lived in a house full of women; Mommy, Grandma Mary, Aunt Rose and a great aunt, Tatha Rose. She was their darling, especially Aunt Rose, who told her stories about riding on rainbows and magical horses with a twisty horn in their foreheads. She asked each of the women in turn where she came from, and the answer was always the same. "You are a child of God." When she asked if God was a name for Mother she was told no. "God is not a female, Beauty. God is our Father. She explored what each of them was feeling when they talked about God, and she realized they knew nothing about Mother. A sad loneliness settled around her as it became harder and harder for her to remember Mother.

Grandma Mary's house had an attic full of mystery. There was a huge feather bed that was used when company came. There were boxes full of letters and pictures and a big trunk full of heavy fabric that she wasn't allowed to open alone. The yard had flowers, a blackberry bush and lots of vegetables. Her favorite place was under a weeping willow tree with branches that came all the way to the ground. She was sitting under the tree one day, telling her doll to be careful not to leave fingerprints on the woodwork, when she heard a voice.

Her secret voice! The one no one else could understand! She jumped up and looked around, and a boy her size swirled into shape as he came out of the tree trunk. Beauty sparkled with excitement as she used her secret voice. "Who are you? Wow, how did you get here? I am called Beauty; what's your name?" "I am called Helper, and I'm part of your Spirit Journey", replied the boy. "And I've always been here, waiting for you to notice me." "But I don't remember a Spirit Journey. There is so much I can't remember." "That's why I'm here," said the boy, "and there are more coming".

With that, another boy and a girl materialized out of the tree trunk. Their names were Shadow and Comfort. All three piped up, taking turns talking and tumbling through sentences as though they shared all their thoughts. "It's very hard to remember your Spirit Journey when you're all alone here. Most people forget before they're even born and it's hardest for them. We're here to help you remember. We can't tell you exactly what it is, but we can help you to remember to keep looking, and we can show you how to look at things differently than most people so you won't miss the signs and patterns that are here to guide you."

The four of them made up games to play, and by thinking about the game, it became real. One day they gathered sticks from the ground and began to turn them into magic wands. As they worked, Helper asked her if she remembered Mother. Beauty felt a start of recognition and a longing, then it faded into sad confusion. She began to cry as the loneliness returned. Comfort wrapped her arms around Beauty and began to sing. The song danced around the four of them like silvery wisps. Beauty watched it swirling and thickening, until finally a pale, lavender rose took form in the middle of the music. There was a silver dew drop on one petal and the scent was heavenly. Each of them touched a petal and breathed deeply, taking in the fragrance of the rose. Shadow came closer to Beauty. "This is a talisman for you. Its purpose is to bring you strength and peace when you need it. I will hide it in the shadows so no one else will notice it. You can get it any time just by asking." Shadow turned slightly, and when he turned back, only silvery wisps remained where the rose had been.

Beauty realized she not only had heard the song, she had also seen its colors and shapes and felt its peace, so this must be a magic song. She was entranced and astounded. "How can I see music and feel music? How can it have color and shape?" "Music exists on many dimensions. That's why it is so powerful," replied Helper. "It will help you remember your Spirit Journey if you listen with all of you, not just your ears. But be careful, there is also dangerous music, which can fill you with feelings of fear and anger. Be careful of the kind of music you let into your being."

Grandma Mary's voice, calling her to lunch, broke the spell of the song, and her friends disappeared into the willow. She sent a soft "thank you" to Comfort for the gift, and to Shadow for protecting her talisman. She began to listen very intently to music, and take careful notice of how it felt in her body, what color it seemed to be, and the shape and movement it contained.

Eventually a girl cousin was born, then siblings of her own, but Beauty spent much of her time alone. Her pretend games were more real to her than the people around her. She still couldn't remember Spirit Journey, but she had the shining one who visited her at night, and wonderful playmates in the willow tree who would do anything with her she wanted, although they came out only when she was alone. Their favorite place to play was under the hanging branches of the willow in the back yard, or under the front porch, behind the wooden steps. One day when Grandma Mary told her about angels, she knew what to call the bright, shining one who came to talk to her sometimes.

One morning while she watched her grandmother make bread dough, Beauty told her grandmother about Shadow and Comfort and Helper, but Beauty's friends frightened Grandma Mary. She said not to talk to them; they might be devils trying to steal her away. But she watched Grandma Mary sit in her garden in the evening and talk to the tiny sparkly ones who helped everything grow. People in the neighborhood said Grandma Mary had the best garden in the world. None of them could grow as much as she did. Grandma Mary said it was the tiny sparkly ones, devas she called them, who came to help because they were asked very politely, and thanked often. Grandma taught Beauty how to talk with them, and how to be very polite. She knew her friends were no more devils than the sparkly ones who worked in the garden, and she wasn't afraid, but she didn't tell anyone else about them.

One day her favorite Aunt Rose brought her a present. It was her very own recording of Peter and the Wolf. The music was wonderful, and made her long to find a forest like the one on the album cover, but in the middle of that forest picture was a dark image of a black and grey wolf. It had red eyes, long, shiny fangs and a very hungry grin. Beauty was frightened of the wolf picture so she kept it turned upside down. She played the music nearly every day, and it always enchanted her. She vividly imagined the forest with all its creatures every time she listened, but tried not to notice the scary wolf. As she listened, she began to realize she could smell the leaves and pine needles of the forest and feel the cool green shadows. As the music played on she began to see and hear chipmunks and squirrels and other small creatures. The wolf was a shadow along the edge of the forest.

Then the wolf started coming into her dreams. It didn't chase her or harm her. The first time it came, it just stared at her for the longest time, and then she woke up. Each time she dreamed of wolf, it came a bit closer, and she could feel a tentative, curious probe. One dreaming day it sniffed her hand, then laid its head next to her on her pillow. The probe was stronger this time, but very gentle. She realized she no longer feared the wolf, and when she rolled over to look at it more closely, its eyes were no longer red-rimmed like the picture. They were soft and brown. When she woke up, she thought it couldn't have been a dream because it was too real.

Eventually Daddy came home from the big ship and Mommy and Daddy moved far away from the rest of the family. The record was forgotten and the wolf dreams stopped after a while, but music contained color and scent and physical feeling from then on. She still spent much of her time alone, and would call Helper and Comfort and Shadow to come out and play. Sometimes they would come, but when they didn't, another person would show up in a few minutes and Beauty would not have any privacy. It was as if they knew when people were coming and stayed away.

One day the four friends were playing a game Aunt Rose had taught her; they were riding on rainbows and catching stardust. Then they would find someone really sad and sprinkle the star dust all around. It seemed to help and made them feel very good. As always, the game was more real to Beauty than any of the rest of her life. She could feel the wind in her face as she slid along a brilliant bow of light, and the laughter they all shared rang in her ears.

Beauty missed the wolf dreams and decided to tell her friends all about them. Maybe it would make the missing dreams more real or even bring them back. She told them about the record and its scary picture, and about how listening to the music carried her to the deep woods and she could feel the life around her and smell the trees. The music had become real to her, just like Comfort's song, and she could hear/feel/see it in many ways. She told them about her dreams, and how the wolf probed gently until she was no longer afraid.

The three listened very intently and when she finished Helper took her hand. "Beauty, pay close attention. These are more than dreams, they are part of your Spirit Journey. If the wolf comes again, ask what its name is. In fact, when you go to bed at night, think about the wolf as hard as you can. See if you can call it the way you call us. You must find out the name." Beauty's eyes were wide at the reminder of Spirit Journey. "Do you suppose the wolf knows Mother?" she whispered with a voice full of longing. "Everyone knows Mother," was the response from Comfort. "And everyone forgets when they first come here."

~~~~~~~~~~~~~~~~

The smoke was rolling into the partially hidden cave. She couldn't breathe so she disobeyed Mother and ran outside. It was so much worse there! Her eyes were streaming so she could hardly see. Her nose and throat burned and she was forced to cough, but taking another breath burned even more. "Mother, where are you?" she called, and her voice was faint and scratchy. Burning debris falling from the trees turned her back as she tried running in one direction then another. **Mother!!** She was really frightened now, and she began getting dizzy from the smoke. Then a pair of strong jaws grasped her just
~~~~~~~~~~~~~~~~

behind the neck, and she went limp with relief as she felt the familiar way Mother carried her.

She was carried around great rocks, past trees beginning to curl with smoke, and once through the middle of a bush already on fire. She lost consciousness on the hot and terrifying journey. She woke up frightened at the smell of smoke, and jumped in panic as she realized it was coming from her own fur. But there was no sign of fire around her. The air was clear and clean, and the terrible heat was gone. She coughed and her mouth was dry and raw, so she took a long drink from the water near her. Then she looked around. She was in the strangest place, like nothing she had ever seen.

The place where she woke up was a bed of dry grass, cut and not attached to the earth. Not possible, not even reasonable, but there it was. There were mounds of it all around. Stranger still, something soared high on all sides, with a top on it, and the land and sky were hidden except for a tall opening just in front of her. A bit of sky and some trees were visible through the opening. She felt trapped and safe at the same time. Nervous, she gnawed at some singed fur, then lapped more water from.... From what? Not a lake or a river, but an odd, small round thing that tipped and spilled on her feet if she tried to step in it. "Where am I? **Mother**?"

Someone new came into the cut grass place, and she bolted in an attempt to hide. Again, she was picked up by powerful jaws at the back of her neck, and went limp as the relaxation reflex took over. She was dropped in the golden grass and the new person gently licked a burned spot on her hip. It felt so soothing. Soon she stopped quivering and looked in the brown eyes just above her. They were soft and kind, not unlike Mother's. She put her mind, her heart and her whole spirit into the question, "Who are you?"

The response was somewhere between a snuffle and a chuckle. She felt welcome. She felt relief in the other one that she would live. She understood there was a language barrier, but that wasn't at all unusual. Mother had taught her she would need to learn many languages so she could speak to all the beings who lived in the forest. The first step to learning a new language was to sense the intentions of the one who is before you. Mother said if you couldn't feel another with your heart, you would never understand what they are saying. For now, her heart felt safe with this new and strange looking creature. She tried speaking with a croak coming from her sore throat. "Did you save me?" The creatures head tilted, and she seemed to smile, then her head nodded up and down.

The creature was large, but not as big as Mother. Her fur was golden-white and very long. So long in fact that it fell over her eyes so one had to peek sideways to see their warm brown depths. When her head tilted in curiosity or compassion, it was easier to get a peek. She had a mate who looked just like her, but a bit larger. The mate had quietly wandered in as they were talking. The mate nuzzled the little cub, gently licked the burned spot, then opened his jaws and took her entire head into his mouth. He made a soft noise deep in his throat and released her with another nuzzle.

"What is your Name, girl child?" asked her rescuer. Fluffy was excited. Their hearts had touched and they could understand each other now. Mother was right! But the question confused her. "What is a name? Is it something you have here in your home? Is it important?" "Of course," came the response. "Everyone has a name. Your name identifies your essence. It tells everyone who they are meeting, and even more importantly, it tells everyone what you have promised to do in your life. When others call you by name, it is a reminder of your promises." The little cub was truly embarrassed. "Mostly I have been called Fluffy. I guess no one thought I would have important promises to make."

"Not at all true! You must be younger than I guessed, and you just haven't had your naming ceremony yet. We will see to it that you have one. For now, let's talk about where you are and why you are here. There was a great forest fire, so great it lit the grasses in the meadow. Some of our sheep were grazing in the meadow closest to the forest and we were sent to bring them home. It was easy to stampede them in the right direction. Sheep are not that smart, and this bunch was scared enough to obey instantly.

We heard a sound coming from the trees, like the cries of our own pups, but somehow different. We couldn't leave so we plunged into the smoke and searched. It didn't take long to find you, running in circles and panicked. I grabbed you and ran behind my mate as he led the way out. We brought you to our home. You look a bit different than our pups, but you feel much the same. Perhaps you can be part of our family and learn our ways and help make our pack stronger. We will teach you how to be one of us, and earn your keep and even be a hero once in a while. Herding sheep is a very important and rewarding job. The pack that herds together stays strong."

They were learning each other's language very quickly. Compassion, kindness and gratitude held all of their hearts open. The little cub asked questions, allowing her pain to be seen.

"But, if I am to do all of this with you, where is Mother? Why isn't she here? She put me in the cave and went out looking for Fuzz Ball. She never came back. Was I wrong to leave the cave? What if she came back and I was gone? Will I never see her again? When I grow big enough, can I go looking for her? Will she know me? Will she want me?"

The big male stepped forward and nuzzled her face. "Your instincts are very good and you were right to leave the cave," he said gently. "If you had stayed there, we wouldn't have found you and you would have died. Who is Fuzz Ball?" "Another small one like me," Fluffy answered, "but a boy. Is he with Mother?" "I can't answer the rest of your questions. Sometimes in great fires like that all the people for miles around die, and sometimes there are miracles and some survive. Your life is a miracle, you know."

"But how will I live alone?" the pup wailed. "I don't even know how to find food yet." "You can stay with us," the female answered. "We will teach you how to work for your food and how to get along with the rest of the pack. We live quite well here, and the work is fun and challenging. We never worry about going hungry. Our pups can be your new brothers and sister, and we will show you how to be a fine sheep dog. We will call you Fluffy until it's time for your naming, and you can call us Mum and Dad." Fluffy determined to do her best in this new pack. She understood the kindness of her rescuers saved her life in more than one way and gratitude filled her.

They raised her with kindness, and tried to teach her to be a member of the family and the extended pack. It should have been easy after all. They each had four legs and a tail and powerful jaws full of teeth. But it just never quite worked. The young wolf pup and the sheep pups could yip and roll and play together, but when they tried to teach her to bark, out would come a howl. Sometimes it was really frustrating for Mum and Dad. Their own pups were coming along OK but this one was different in just enough ways that they sometimes felt like failures.

It was not that anyone was unkind. She just didn't seem to really belong. Then, when she was old enough to be sent to sheep dog training, the loneliness grew. She looked too different. Her howl was not a welcome sound. Her teachers made it clear that her howling was against the natural order of things; dangerous in fact. She would have to be punished if she kept it up. She might be strange looking, but after all she was an adopted sheep dog and howling simply wasn't done. Particularly not by a female.

Fluffy had to learn to work like the others and help the dog pack get enough food and keep the sheep rounded up and other animals away, but more and more of the time she was left to spend alone. But the worst thing of all for Fluffy was that she was beginning to forget Mother. She tried remembering the things Mother had taught her, but many were slipping away. What if Mother came back some day and they didn't recognize each other? Why couldn't she remember her scent? The only thing she was really sure of any more was the language of the heart Mother had taught her. It was easy to remember that because Mum and Dad knew it and spoke it with her.

In spite of the difficulty that Fluffy and her pack had adjusting to each other, it was apparent to all that she was very bright and very fast. She excelled in sheep school and before long could turn a herd of sheep with speed and precision even the adults couldn't match. She seemed to sense which sheep would try to break away just before it happened, which lamb would get confused and fall behind, which ram would get aggressive. At times it looked like she might actually be having a conversation with the sheep, guiding them and chastising them easily. But the pack was certain sheep didn't talk, so that probably wasn't possible.

Her siblings and peers grumbled. It wasn't fair for her to get so much praise because she happened to be bigger and faster, and they would sometimes snub her. But the adults knew a great sheep dog when they saw one. The pack would thrive! But the howling remained a problem.

One day, as the sun was setting, the pups were playing in the cut grass place, and the play began to get rough. One nipped a bit too hard, another nipped back, the yips and whines grew louder, and then Fluffy growled. Everyone stopped playing, hackles raised. Several of the pups began circling and joined the growling, while others ran for cover. Tension was mounting and the instinct for domination rose quickly. Fluffy and four other pups were not backing down, their heads lowered threateningly. Mum bounded in and whacked two of them out of the circle, and the rest ran before she could get to them. The tension was broken and the pups sniffed each other and half heartedly began playing again. The incident ended peacefully and was never repeated, but they were never as much at ease with each other again. Something had shifted and innocence was lost.

Lessons in the Sun

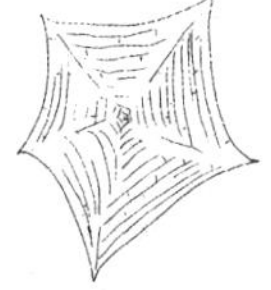

Learn to see, and then you'll know that there is no end to the new worlds of our vision.

Carlos Castaneda

One morning Beauty woke up and Mommy was gone. Aunt Rose had come to stay with her, but she was frightened anyway. Aunt Rose explained Mommy had gone to the hospital to get her a baby sister, and she would come right back home as soon as she found the proper one. That soothed Beauty, and she and Aunt Rose began to make plans for the new baby. Mommy would take care of the baby just like Beauty took care of her baby doll. They could do it together and that sounded like a fun game. She might even get to hold the baby. It would be bigger than her doll, but much smaller than her.

That was pleasing. It was about time there was someone around here smaller than her. She could teach her new sister the things she had learned. A vague thought passed through Beauty's mind. "Will she remember Mother, and her Spirit Journey, and maybe even mine?" She thought about the wolf dreams and her friends. She was thinking about Spirit Journey and Mother more than she had in a very long time. She tried every night to call the wolf to her dreams, but nothing had happened yet. She would tell the new baby as well, and see what she thought.

When Mommy came home with her new sister, Beauty rushed to talk to her in the special language she shared with her friends and angel, but something was wrong. The baby just cried and fussed and couldn't seem to hear Beauty at all. In fact, Beauty couldn't understand her either. The baby didn't have the special language. She wouldn't be able to teach her the things she had learned. She couldn't even ask her about Mother and her Spirit Journey. Beauty felt more alone than ever.

One day, Mommy seemed very unhappy. The baby was crying a lot more than usual. Dinner started to burn as Mommy tried to quiet the crying child, which is when Mommy started crying. Beauty tugged at her skirt. "Mommy, let me hug you and make it all better. Mommy, I'll give you kisses. Bend over Mommy. Let me hug you." But Mommy pushed her away and yelled, "Stop it!" Then she took the baby in the bedroom with her and slammed the door shut.

Beauty threw herself across the cheap plastic hassock in the living room and cried and cried. She cried for a very long time, and no one paid any attention. Then she heard a wailing voice inside her saying over and over again, "I don't care. I hate you. I don't care." Soon she was wailing the words aloud. "I don't love you, I hate you. I don't care, I don't care."

Finally the baby went to sleep and Mommy came out. She was irritated with the messy puddle Beauty had made on the plastic hassock with her tears and runny nose. She cleaned up the mess with rough motions and Beauty choked back her sobs. There were no hugs and kisses that day. Something felt very broken. That night when Mommy came to say goodnight, Beauty curled up in the other direction, pretending she was asleep. She didn't remember to ask for her rose talisman.

Not long after that, a visiting relative from another town said to her, "My you're growing into such a big girl, Beauty. How old are you?" "Older than the earth" Beauty replied heavily, although she had no idea what that meant. The relative said "that's so silly, honey. You are just a little girl."

~~~~~~~~~~~~~~~~

It was the first hot day of the year. Mommy was cleaning their second floor apartment and she was very irritated at being so hot and sweaty. Or maybe she was irritated because Beauty was asking her questions and pestering her for snacks. She gave the girl a cookie and sent her out to play. "Don't go too far. Make sure you can hear when I call." "OK, Mommy, I promise." Of course the promise was broken in minutes. Not that she meant to, but there was so much to see and each new thing just led to another delight.

She was walking on a rutted, one lane dirt road that led only to the railroad tracks and had no cars or people on it. It was one of her favorite places to explore. The road had thick, green bushes and small trees lining it, and if you went all the way to the railroad tracks, the trees were tall and blocked most of the sun. When Beauty walked along the tracks, sometimes she had to crawl to squeeze through the undergrowth. She got more dirty than usual on those days, and Mommy would scold her, but it was worth it.

She felt like she could hear whispers in the woods, but couldn't make sense of them, even when she tried very hard. The sounds felt welcoming and friendly so she kept trying. There was an old root cellar in the woods, its door and steps all that remained of what had once been a farm house. Beauty had not yet found the courage to go down the steps into the damp and dusky room.
~~~~~~~~~~~~~~~~

She was headed for the tracks when suddenly, sparkling in the sunlight in front of her was a huge spider web, reaching all the way across the narrow road. She saw it just in time to keep from running into it, and she felt a little scared. Someone had told her spiders were dangerous and could make you die, or at least get very sick. It was probably Uncle Elmer. He seemed to like to scare her. He would tell her something awful, then laugh when she ran and hid her face in Mommy's lap.

Beauty backed a few steps away from the spider web and felt safer. She spotted a large round spider on it, but it was busy rolling something into a ball with more web strands. She got dirty, as usual, sitting cross legged in the dust, and watched the spider work. It was so interesting and the spider was so good at making web strands and using them. She noticed how wonderfully balanced everything was, and how with each movement of the spider, the entire web would shift and wave, as if in a breeze. She thought that must be as much fun for the spider as carnival rides were for her.

"Hello Beauty", a voice said. It was one of those voices, like her invisible friends. She heard it in her mind, not with her ears. A question rippled out of her cells. "Who said that?" "I did. I want to thank you for being careful and not ruining my web. It took a long time to make." The girl looked up and the spider was no longer rolling things into balls. It was sitting very still and looking directly at her. "Is that really you talking to me? A spider?" "Why not" was the response. "We're both children of the earth, aren't we? We should be able to talk with each other."

"Wow" said Beauty, with all the energy in her cells of course, not her human voice. "This is as good as my bestest friends who come to play with me. Their names are Helper and Shadow and Comfort. Helper talks to me about my Spirit Journey, but I still can't remember it much. Shadow talks to me about places to hide, and Comfort says I can call her any time I feel lonesome. I've just had kid friends and angel friends so far, but you could be my friend too. Just promise not to bite me. Will you tell me your name? Will you show me where you go in the winter? My mommy makes me stay in, mostly. Do you have other friends? How do you make that web?"

"Hold on little one. One thing at a time. First, I only bite when I am in danger or when I have to gather food. You are not food for me, so that's not an issue. If you are careful about not breaking spider webs, none of us will bite you because there will be no danger. That's why I wanted to thank you. When I first saw you, I thought there might be danger, but you were careful so everything is fine. It's important for children of the earth to respect each other and do no harm."

That made sense to Beauty, except for one thing. "Spider, you called me little one, but I am ever so much bigger than you. Why did you call me that?" The spider did the spiderly equivalent of taking a very deep breath. "You don't start with the easy questions, do you child? First you want to know my name, and now you ask about the most important thing all children of the earth need to learn. What I have to tell you is that the size of your body does not count for much. It's the size of your spirit that matters. You are very young as human life goes, and your spirit, which is wise in other places, is just beginning to grow in understanding of this earth. I am getting old as spider lives go, and my spirit is nearly complete. So, to me, you are a little one."

"Oh," Beauty responded dejectedly. "You're just like my family. I'm too little to understand so nobody will explain anything to me." "Not true at all", insisted Spider. "You are the only human of any size I have ever spoken with. I only speak with you because your spirit is big enough to understand. I just meant its earth form isn't yet as big as its going to be one day."

"So, does that mean you will be my friend? Will you talk to me some more and tell me your name?" asked the girl. "I already am your friend, and we can talk often, and I will tell you my name after you discover your own true name," replied spider. "You must have a naming ceremony in order to understand the value and meaning of a name." "But, you said you are old!" Beauty cried. "What if you don't live long enough to talk to me after my naming ceremony?" She could feel Spider smile. "I will be there. I promise."

They talked for a long while. Spider explained that her web was more than just a place to catch food and raise her young. "Beauty, if you look closely at this web, you will see that it is perfectly balanced. Every point where it is connected helps make the whole web stronger, and every strand is so resilient that if some of them are broken, the rest of the web survives. If you can learn to make your life like my web, with every strand contributing to the whole and all of it resilient and flexible, you will grow a very great spirit. The time may even come when you teach other humans how to build a spirit life."

"That's very kind of you to say" replied Beauty, "but no one listens to me. They call me a silly little girl, or sometimes they say I have to grow up and stop talking such foolishness. They tell me my imagination is running away with me and if I don't stop it people will begin to think I don't tell the truth."

"You will grow up my friend, and when you do you will know the difference between foolishness and speaking the truth you discover on your Spirit Journey," said Spider. Lights went off in the young girl's mind.

"Spirit Journey?" She had to ask him! "What is that? I feel like I should know and it feels right when you say that or when Helper talks about it, but I can't quite see it. What is my Spirit Journey?"

"You will remember perfectly when it's time", replied the web weaver. "Just keep asking questions and if people make fun of you, remember not everyone can hear spiders and secret friends and angels, so they just don't understand what you are talking about. It doesn't mean you are wrong, but you may have to learn not to share everything you know all the time. Shadow can tell you more about that. That's called wisdom." They talked a little longer, then it was time for her to go home. She could tell by where the sun shone. "Bye Spider friend. I'll come back tomorrow and I promise to be careful of all the webs."

Beauty skipped home, pausing only to pick some sweet, wild honeysuckle for Mommy, then skipped up the stairs. Mommy was humming as she turned fried chicken in a pan. Cooking usually made her happy. She smiled as Beauty held out the flowers, then sighed in exasperation as she looked at her very dirty daughter. "Why can't you stay clean like your cousin? Let's get you in the tub before Daddy gets home. He's going to want to see a clean, pretty daughter, not this grimy tomboy." "Do you like the flowers, Mommy?" Beauty asked. "Yes dear, now get in the water." Mommy was really in a good mood. She smiled and brought toy plastic buckets and cups for her to play with as she soaked, and added bubble bath under the stream of water. Beauty sighed with contentment.

It had been such a wonderful day that she didn't even get tense when the baby started crying after dinner. Mommy picked up the baby and Daddy let her help with the dishes. She remembered "wisdom" and didn't talk about her conversation with Spider when Daddy asked her about her day. She just told him about the beautiful web sparkling in the sun, and how she had been so careful not to run into it. When bed time came, Mommy read to her, then kissed her goodnight and tucked her in. What a perfect day this had been.

Conversations with the spider continued that summer. They talked several times about how the web was similar to the web of energy that was her life, and even could be looked upon as the web of all of life. They talked about the power of the web, and its many uses. They talked about its misuse and what that might do to the whole. One day spider told Beauty to sit just so, and let the strands of the web, sparkling in the sun, fill her whole vision. As she did, the background faded into a fuzzy blur and the web stood out bright and beautiful. "Watch closely," whispered spider from a corner of the web. After a time, a tiny insect flew over the web. Spider sent out a silvery strand and captured the insect, then began rolling it in a ball. Finally the ball was attached to a small space in one corner.

"There are many lessons in what I just did," said spider. "Can you name one?" Beauty carefully considered her reply. "One lesson could be that what you need is nearby and you just have to take advantage of it. Let's see, you don't have to take what belongs to someone else. There's enough in the world just for you. Oh, I know. You have to take care of it and place it where it won't get lost. That would be wasteful." "Great" said spider. "What else." Silence. More silence. "OK, here's a hint. What if I had no web when I threw my silvery strand? No place to stand, and no place to store what I've caught. What then?" Ideas began to click in her mind. "With no place to stand you might have slipped and missed. Even if you didn't miss, it would be hard to roll the ball. Then where would you put it? On your back, but that would slow you down terribly. On a tree or a leaf, but then anyone could take it. And you would have nowhere to feed your young."

"Excellent, you're getting the idea. Everything leads to everything else, and whether or not you have a strong foundation will determine how easy or difficult your life will be." "But I don't make webs," said Beauty. "What is my foundation?" "Of course you do! The web of your life is an energy pattern, as real as my web and much stronger, even though few can see it. Every thought, every choice, every action you take either adds another strong strand to your web, or it breaks one. Remember how you were careful not to break my web the first time we met? You must be every bit as careful with your web. This is true of all of life, but few remember it. This lesson is an important part of remembering your Spirit Journey."

Just then another very large spider dropped onto the web and moved toward the silvery balls that were stored for her friend's offspring. Spider retreated to a far corner, raised up and began to fling her silvery strands at the intruder. At first the strands were just brushed aside, but as they came faster and faster, began to stick here and there. Spider gave the whole thing a jerk and the intruder was captured, legs tangled in iron strong silver. When the rolling was completed, spider took the ball to the edge of the web, lowered it on another strand, and finished by tying it to a tree a distance away. Beauty's heart felt the trembling weariness of her friend after the battle, and sent a beam of love and support toward her.

Spider looked at her with surprise. "Thank you for that, I feel much better." Beauty's eyes filled with tears. "Oh, Spider, I was so afraid you would be hurt and I didn't know how to stop that ugly spider. I don't have the right kind of silver threads to catch it and wrap it." "Yes, you do. You already know how to send out your silvery threads. We just haven't practiced how to use them when you are in danger. Now you know they can carry anything from love to death. Remember you can send love and support to any of your friends this way, and it's also the same thing you use to raise and care for your young. Change your intention and your energy patterns become your defense. Just remember, choosing to use them for harm when you or those you love are in no danger will cause great harm to your own web of life. You will become weaker, not stronger.

"Meanwhile you have witnessed the importance of a strong foundation, and the fact that you have the right to do whatever it takes to send dangerous intruders away. Do as little harm as possible, but if you are attacked in the future, put whatever kind of energy you need into the silvery thread you throw at those who would harm you. Wrap them tightly and fasten them to something strong." Beauty sighed. "But who would hurt a little girl? I'm not dangerous."

For a moment it felt like Spider had put hands on her shoulders and was shaking her. The message was intense and very loud. "Never forget that you are only little on the outside. Even if you grow into a great and powerful woman, the only thing that ever counts is how big you are on the inside. There are many today who can sense what you are on the inside and they don't want anything like that on this earth. You too can feel what others are on the inside. Trust that feeling more than anything else."

The girl was crying softly now. "Oh, Spider, why won't people like me? What's wrong with me?" She could feel a spiderly sigh. It blew compassion across her heart. "Little one, there is nothing wrong with you. It's just that many people have allowed fear to close their eyes and ears, and you remind them of what they fear. I know you are lonely, but you will find more and more companions to share your journey. I promise."

Traveling Companions

A real friend is one who walks in when the rest of the world walks out.

Walter Winchell

The pack was curled up on the dry cut grass, in the place that hid most of the sky. They had romped and tussled at the end of the day and now sleep had overcome them. Some of them were piled in a heap, snoring together, and some were sprawled nearby. Fluffy slept with them sometimes, particularly when she was cold, but most nights she wandered off on her own. Tonight she had found a big rock, still warm from the daytime sun, with a bunch of soft, real grass around it. Not the cut stuff. She stretched in luxury, then curled up next to the rock, watching the night lights. The great night light was a sliver tonight, making all the tiny lights look brighter than ever.

The tiny lights called to her somehow, triggering an ancient memory that she didn't really understand. It was almost as if she could follow them somewhere. But where? There was home, the fields and spaces where she lived, and there was the burned forest, still a place of fear, although seasons had passed since the fire. Where else was there? Is there a where else? Fluffy grew drowsy and fell asleep wondering where the tiny lights might lead.

A beautiful goose landed next to Fluffy, startling her awake. "Hi, I'm called Traveler. What is your name?" "UH, folks call me Fluffy." "Well, I can see you're about to outgrow that silly moniker. You look much more sleek than fluffy. Say, I've got an itch to go exploring. Come fly with me. We could have a great time." "Hold on," said Fluffy. "I've never seen anyone like you before. How do you know my language? How can we be talking together?"

"It's the language of the heart of course, silly. I could hear you wondering about the stars and I love exploring so I had to come invite you along. I knew you wouldn't hurt me because we share this language and I could see your gentleness. My parents finished raising me and have moved on with their lives and I don't have a mate yet so it's kind of lonely for me. Would you be my friend and go flying and exploring with me?"

This was so over the top for Fluffy she nearly exploded with questions. "But I don't know how to fly! And is there anywhere to fly to? Could I find my way back if I did know how to fly? And isn't it scary to fly up high above the ground? I could fall and get killed, couldn't I? Well, none of those questions really matter, because I don't know how to fly, so I guess I can't come with you."

Traveler ruffled his feathers and flapped his wings. He seemed to be grinning a bit. "Well, I can help you with that my friend. You see, I'm not just an ordinary goose. I, uh, well, I have a bit of magic in me, and I can do things other geese can't. For instance, even though it looks like you are larger than me, I can shape shift enough so you could ride on my back as I fly. We could explore the other places the lights in the sky point to. We could have a great adventure!" Fluffy's eyes were huge with astonishment.

"Oh and by the way," Traveler continued, "I never get lost. Once I have been somewhere, I can always find my way back. That's not even the magical part of me. Any goose can do that. I could teach you how to always find your way back if you like."

"But, but what if I fall off your back?" stammered Fluffy. "I could get killed." Traveler assured her, "You won't fall off, and even if you did I would just swoop under you and catch you. I can fly faster than you can fall, so you will be perfectly safe. Besides, don't you have to go on a great adventure and discover your purpose, so you can get your real name? Staying just "Fluffy" all your life would be really limiting. We can explore forests beyond the burned part, mountain ranges and even oceans."

"Wow, I can't believe this is happening to me," Fluffy bleated, sounding almost sheepish. "Are there really more forests, and what are mountains, and what on earth is ocean? How is this possible?" Traveler leaned forward and said, in a conspiratorial whisper, "Magic! Hop on."

Fluffy had a strange sensation as she climbed on to Traveler's back, which had plenty of room for her in spite of the goose being so much smaller. She gasped and her heart pounded as powerful wings launched them into the air. She watched the huge dry grass place get smaller and smaller as Traveler circled the meadow, and then they flew straight over the short stumps of the burned forest. It hadn't occurred to her to question how she could see so well in the dark.

"Hey Fluffy," Traveler called. "Where do you want to go? Pick a star to follow." The tiny lights looked much brighter from up here. Fluffy felt even more strongly that they were calling to her. "That one" said Fluffy, pointing to a star that was pulsing with light about half way to the horizon. "OK, here we go" said Traveler. Fluffy wobbled a bit as Traveler adjusted course and picked up speed, but she didn't fall off. She wondered about feeling the call of the stars. Was there a heart language she could learn so she could talk with them as well? But, how could these little lights have a heart? The lights at home were either bonfires or torches, or the hard, slick things that only The People could turn on or off. None of those lights had a heart, and no one in her pack liked to get too close to any of them.

They flew in silence for a while, then Traveler landed at the edge of a small lake. "Let's take a break and have a drink of water," said Traveler. This is one of my favorite spots and we're not in any hurry so let's enjoy ourselves here for a bit." Fluffy had the same strange sensation as she climbed off Traveler's back and found herself standing next to a bird that was tiny compared to her. She shivered a bit, and then noticed the water was stationary in one place, not running like the streams and rivers of her earliest memories. It was like the water in the container in the dry grass place, but many, many times bigger. She gingerly stepped into the edge, half expecting it to tip and slosh like the water container at home. But it remained steady as she stood in the water and drank her fill.

Traveler was yards away from the shore, diving and preening and shaking his feathers. Fluffy could hear him whoop and chuckle with delight. She sniffed around, wandering away from the lake and nearing the woods that surrounded the meadow. The woods were green and beautiful, with no sign of fire. She jumped and her hackles rose as a long, deep howl burst across the quiet night air. Her heart in her throat, she surrendered to the impulse to howl, and called out her richest sound ever. It felt so good, she did it again.

Her ears picked up nearly silent foot falls coming fast through the woods and she started backing away. A huge grey wolf leaped out of the forest, landing just a few feet from her. He began circling and sniffing, slowly coming closer and closer. Fluffy tried to feel this one with her heart, to see if they could talk to each other. A very strange feeling was coming from him. Something was pulsing, WANT! WANT! and Fluffy felt trapped and frightened. As she attempted to dodge, he edged closer, growling. She growled back and that seemed to amuse him. WANT! WANT!

In a whirl of flapping wings, Traveler landed in front of her. "Hop on, quick." Fluffy dove on, hardly noticing the strange sensation this time, and Traveler launched them skyward so hard he nearly dumped her. The big grey leaped after them, jaws snapping, and just missed batting them down with his paw. He stared after them for a moment and then slunk off into the woods. "Whew," said Traveler, "that was too close. I didn't realize you were nearly old enough to mate until I heard your howl. That was a beauty, I tell you! You're nearly a grown wolf. We're going to have to be more careful or some big guy will steal you away before I get to teach you anything."

"Steal me away! Why?" cried Fluffy. "To have you as a mate, of course. One day I will have a goose mate and one day you will have a wolf mate." "Oh, I don't think so" was her shaky reply. "That guy felt awful and scary. I think I'll skip that mating business and just travel and take care of sheep. And why are you calling me wolf? My Mum and Dad are sheepdogs, and so am I. Everyone says I look funny and they don't like my howl, but I'm really good at rounding up sheep."

Traveler looked thoughtful for a few minutes, then asked in a gentle voice, "Fluffy, where were you born?" "In a small cave in the forest, before the big fire. Then

Mum and Dad found me and took me to their home and raised me." "Who was with you in the cave, before the fire?" was the next question. "**M-m-mother**, but I don't like to think about her because I miss her so much when I do. She taught me the language of the heart. She was sleek and powerful, and had rich brown eyes and a wonderful howl." "Just like you," said Traveler softly. "You were born a wolf." Fluffy let out one mournful howl, then they traveled in silence for a long while.

The next time they stopped to rest, the companions were very quiet, careful not to attract any attention. They each found a secluded spot and snuggled in for a nap. They woke up to a bright, warm morning, hungry and thirsty. Traveler set to munching water plants along the inside of a small stream. Fluffy caught a few voles. Not a very satisfying meal, but it helped. They heard a crying sound, and followed it to find a small child in soggy, sagging pants behind a large rock. It was dirt covered, tear streaked, and smelled rather awful.

Fluffy tested for a heart, and found one that was frightened and hungry, but it knew something about heart language. "What's the matter?" asked Fluffy. The child stopped crying and tilted its head in curiosity. "Who are you? Why are you crying?" The child took a shuddering, deep breath and Fluffy heard "lost." Traveler joined them and said, "Lost is he? That's too bad. Well, we'd better get going. There's not enough food here for us to eat well.

Fluffy was incensed. "We can't just leave him here. At least I can't. I know how bad it was to be lost once, and we've got to help him get home." Traveler ruffled his feathers irritably. "How are we supposed to do that? We don't even know where he lives, and even if we did, what makes you think he'll follow us?" "I find lost sheep all the time by their scent," Fluffy answered. "This one smells really strong, so his trail should be easy to follow. I'll sniff my way along, and you flap your wings or something to urge him to follow." Traveler grumbled, but he helped, sometimes flapping his wings and sometimes nipping at the boy's soggy drawers.

They walked a long time. Sometimes the boy would just stop, lay down and go to sleep. Traveler and Fluffy took turns sleeping and standing guard. Once Fluffy was startled awake as Traveler squawked at an approaching snake. She checked the snake's heart and found it was only looking for a warm rock to have a nap, and meant no harm. They agreed to treat each other with respect, and the three strange companions went on their way.

Eventually they came to a clearing with a house in the center. "Stop!" warned Traveler. "Don't go any closer; it's dangerous." "Don't be silly," protested Fluffy. "The bad smell I'm using for scent is leading right there." "Fluffy", yelled Traveler, "that's a People place, and The People kill wolves, especially if they see you with one of their young. They won't believe you brought him home. They'll just think you stole him." "Some of them must have the language of the heart. I'll speak to them and show them how gentle I am," insisted Fluffy. Traveler was getting frightened now. "The People don't have the language of the heart. They won't be able to hear you." "But Traveler, this young one can speak it, a little." Traveler sighed in exasperation. "They lose it when they grow up. I have never met an adult People with the language of the heart, have you?" "Well, no," admitted Fluffy. "But we can't just leave him here. It's still too far for him."

At that moment, two half-grown People came out of the house, climbed on the back of a small pony and headed in their direction. "Bucky look!" exclaimed the girl. "Isn't that a wolf?" Her brother answered in a panic, "Yes, and there's baby Matt right next to it! We've got to go get Dad!" "Wait! Wait! We can't leave Matt sitting there alone. What if the wolf drags him away again. I'm sure that's what happened. It's a miracle he's alive. We have to do something!" she wailed, as tears of panic filled her eyes. Little Matt chose that moment to start bellowing at the top of his lungs. The wolf howled. Amazingly a big goose flew up in the air above them, honking and flapping his wings.

The young People edged their pony closer, and the wolf backed away. Dad had heard the ruckus and was running their way, clutching a rifle. The pony edged closer, the goose flapped and honked with all his might, and Fluffy backed farther away. "I don't think the wolf means any harm" said the girl in awed tones. "Run! Run!" screamed Traveler. "A People with a gun is almost here. Run for your life, Fluffy!" Traveler dove at the man's head, nipping him painfully, and distracted him for crucial moments. "Dad! Dad! Matt is safe," yelled the two on the pony. At that, the man dropped his rifle and scooped up his screaming son. He hugged the baby, thrust him at the two older children, went for a horse and grabbed his rifle, heading for the woods with a burning determination to kill the dangerous wolf.

Fluffy was covering a lot of ground with a mile gobbling lope. Traveler finally caught up with her at the stream and they paused for a drink. "Here get on, quick," panted Traveler. "That guy is riding a horse fast and he's got kill energy pouring out of his eyes." Fluffy got on with a shudder and they soared. The man with the rifle saw a strangely shaped goose and caught it in the crosshairs of his gun. Then he decided not to shoot. He would save all his bullets for that marauding wolf.

Traveler flew and flew, crossing hills and valleys and rivers, until he was sure the man would stop and not go that far past his own territory. The exhausted goose landed near a small stream and slowly sipped water as his panting eased. He took a few bites of water grass, and fell over, sound asleep. Fluffy drank deeply, keeping a sharp watch around them. She caught a squirrel, then a rabbit, and it almost was enough to ease her hunger. She thought being out in the open might be dangerous so she gently picked up Traveler in her strong jaws and carried him into a thicket. She pushed leaves into a soft pile and lay down on it, pulling Traveler close to her chest for warmth. He trembled and twitched, but he slept deeply.

Fluffy thought about their adventures and realized Traveler had saved her life and her freedom at the risk of his own. He was wise in the ways of the world and very quick to take action when there was danger. "How is it possible," thought Fluffy, "that he knows so much more than I do, and he's just a young one like me? Is it because he grew up with his own Mother who taught him wild ways? Will I ever learn to find enough food and to get out of danger like he does? And why did he risk his life for me? Will I ever be as smart and as kind as Traveler?" She remembered Traveler asking her to be his friend – was that just two days ago? – and realized Traveler was truly her friend. She felt gratitude for her friend fill her heart and as drowsiness claimed her, she asked one more question. "Will I ever be able to return his kindness?"

As Fluffy drifted off to sleep, she dreamed of a young female People sleeping on a narrow bed. She was strongly drawn to the girl and cautiously approached her. The young girl opened her eyes with a blink of recognition. Wanting to know if the girl knew the language of the heart, she sent out a gentle probe. It seemed she did because she could understand the girl's wondering about who this was visiting her. Fluffy gently sniffed the girl's hands, then laid her head next to the girl on her pillow and slept soundly.

First Test

Freedom is actually a bigger game than power. Power is about what you can control. Freedom is about what you can unleash.

Harriet Rubin

Every summer Beauty and her sister were taken back to Chicago to stay with Grandma Mary for two weeks while Mommy and Daddy went on vacation. Grandma Mary and Aunt Rose and Great Aunt Tatha Rose all still lived in the same house, and made a great fuss over the two girls. Beauty loved going there. There were trips to Lake Michigan and to the beautiful museums filled with astonishing marvels. Aunt Rose took her downtown for concerts and ballet performances. Aunt Rose was a very sophisticated single city lady and in the summer refused to date any man who wouldn't welcome her niece along on the date. Often the evenings would end in an elegant bar or restaurant and the marvelous treat of a Shirley Temple, with a cherry in it, topped off the night.

Even better, her friends met her under the willow tree every day and they had great adventures together, many of them inspired by the story telling of Aunt Rose. One day she told them about the terrible day with mommy when there were no kisses, and how miserable she had been when she fell asleep alone.

“Oh Beauty,” said Shadow. “I was waiting right there in the dark with your talisman. Why didn’t you ask for the rose so it could comfort you?” “I don’t know,” Beauty explained.” “I just never thought of it.” Comfort hugged her and replied, “We can’t come to you unless you call us. And the only reason we wouldn’t appear is if there are people nearby who wouldn’t understand.” Helper piped in. “Sometimes when you call, we can help you even if we have to stay invisible. We can do *things* with time and space, and sometimes tickle a human mind with an idea they might not have on their own. One day you will be strong enough and not need us, but until then please call us any time. We will do anything we can.”

Much of Beauty’s loneliness was eased, and she spent warm afternoons with her three friends. She told them about Spider and all she had taught her. They were suitably impressed. Spider was a powerful ally and very few humans were graced by spiderly help. She practiced calling for her rose with Shadow, and all four of them delighted in the intoxicating sweetness of its scent. Comfort taught her how to fill a sad memory with the color and smell of the rose, and it helped soften her sadness about mommy. “So,” said Helper. “You have friends and allies, you have learned about silver strands and the web of life. You have a talisman. Does that help you remember your Spirit Journey?” Beauty thought carefully for a moment, then shook her head no with a small sigh.

~~~~~~~~~~~~~~~~

Grandma Mary got up early every morning to make bread, and once she had it in the oven would walk down the block to go to church while it was baking. She went every single day, and would take Beauty if she was up and
~~~~~~~~~~~~~~~~

dressed. But Beauty's favorite time with Grandma Mary was the evening processions.

On a week night the priest would walk through the streets, chanting prayers as some men followed him, carrying a statue of the Blessed Virgin on their shoulders. Beauty understood it was just a statue, but somehow she was stirred by it, as though it was reminding her of something very special. Beauty tried talking to it with her private language but it didn't answer.

"Oh," she heard, and she felt a start of surprise coming from somebody in the small crowd. She tried talking again, but the only thing that came back was an anxious sense of fear. She couldn't tell who had heard her, and the person certainly wasn't talking. Then she felt a wave of deep sadness coming from someone, and thought about how sad she would be without her private language. Beauty used her wisdom and it seemed she shouldn't tell anyone about this and she shouldn't try to find the sad person.

The procession started to move and almost all of the attention was focused on the priest and the statue. Some of the boys wore funny white shirts with lace on them and swung brass pots on chains. Sweet smelling smoke came out of the pots. Some of the girls walked just in front of the statue with the boys, tossing flower petals out of baskets. The older girls and boys were flirting a little, the girls suppressing giggles and the boys elbowing each other as they pretended not to notice.

All the women and girls had scarves or lace hankies covering their heads. Men and women followed the statue, carrying candles and chanting prayers with the priest. Beauty thought she could feel something more during those processions. It was as though she knew each person better, and sensed their happiness or their sadness. Many of the adults weren't grown up at all, and were confused about their lives, not knowing what to do or how to be. She could tell they didn't remember Mother, and had no idea of a Spirit Journey.

But the statue seemed to call to many of them as a reminder. Perhaps they walked in the processions every week seeking what they had lost. All of them seemed to have a deep sense of connection to each other that moved out beyond the summer evening and the chanting. It reminded Beauty of spider webs, sparkling in the sun. It felt very good, and she had a fleeting glimpse of Spirit Journey. Somehow this was connected.

The sense of rightness and connection stayed with Beauty. As she thought about the priest who led everyone and chanted the prayers, her heart would fill and she could see herself growing up and being the priest. She already knew a lot about how to weave things together. Spider had taught her that you can weave shining spirit strands of people, of ideas, of good feelings, and many other things. When she watched the priest she could see him doing it, and she felt very grown up knowing she could do it too.

The next week when the neighborhood people were gathering at the church to start the procession, Beauty noticed a new family had joined them. They didn't look happy like most of the others, and they spoke to no one. The mommy pushed her daughter to the front of the line to grab a big handful of flowers before any of the other girls got any. For the first time, there wasn't enough for all the girls carrying baskets.

Beauty didn't really mind. She decided to walk right near the priest and help him weave these new people into the shining strands shared by all the rest of the neighborhood. The priest smiled at her, but he didn't seem to be able to hear or speak the special language. "But what a great web weaver", Beauty thought aloud. She jumped right in to helping him weave the strands.

It hit her like a wall of iron. The hard, cold blow brought her down fast, and she propped herself on her hands and knees in the street, reeling with shock. Suddenly it was utterly silent and no one seemed to be moving. No one, except the new family.

They were walking toward her, waves of anger rippling out of them. The girl was gray and colorless. There didn't seem to be any life force in her, just anger. The man was red in the face with rage and the woman.....the very center of her being was a black, bottomless hole. Beauty looked desperately to the priest, then to her Grandma Mary for help, but they were as motionless as everyone else. At the last possible minute, Beauty remembered her friend the spider and all the lessons on weaving. She remembered Spider throwing a shining strand to catch a fly, then spinning it round and round until it was helpless, then attaching it securely to the web. Spider had taught her to focus on her solar plexus and imagine power surging and shining, waiting for her to direct it with her mind.

She quickly focused on her center and found a shimmering ball there. She tossed a strand to the man then spun it around him as fast as she could, and pinned him to a tree. She ignored the girl, turning her attention to the dark woman who was almost on her, and tossed her a strand, but couldn't make it spin. She tossed her another, then another, and they each went into the deep, black hole at her center. The woman stopped coming closer and pulled at the strands. Beauty threw them by handfuls now, until the black hole began to steam and glow. The woman screamed, collapsed in a heap and suddenly disappeared in a crack of sound and smoke. The young girl moaned, then began to cry dry, racking sobs.

Beauty's head was reeling, and she was quivering with exhaustion and fear. The procession came back to life and Grandma Mary rushed up. "Honey, you've really skinned your knees, oh, and look at that bump on your head! What ever made you trip like that? Let's get you home right now and get you cleaned up and bandaged." Grandma Mary kept talking in soothing tones. She was sure Father Joe would understand if they left right away, and anyway Beauty wasn't one of the flower girls, and maybe there would be a special snack at home after she was bandaged. Beauty looked around nervously, but the strangers were gone and nobody else seemed to have noticed anything. She breathed a ragged sigh and turned to go home with Grandma Mary.

It was right there, nearly on top of her! Not the woman, just the black hole. Again, nothing else was moving. She used all of the power in her special language and screamed NO! Another voice joined her, screaming NO! in the special language. The two of them kept screaming as they watched the black hole dwindle and turn into a small tornado shape and burrow down into the city street. Beauty was standing next to an ordinary looking woman. Both of them were shaking with the effort of their battle. She shook Beauty and warned her to stop using the special language. "Every time you do, they will come and try to kill you. You have to stop using it like I did, and stop listening to anyone who does use it. It's not allowed here, and you will die if you keep doing this." The woman turned and walked away and the procession came back to life. Grandma was chatting about having a treat as they walked toward home. Beauty shivered, and a wave of sorrow tightened her throat as she quietly followed Grandma Mary home.

That night at bedtime, she pulled the sheet over her head, even though it was stuffy and hot in her attic room.

She focused her attention as hard as she could and called Shadow so she could have the sweetness of her talisman to ease her sadness. She called and called, and finally the lovely sent of the flower filled the air. The scent rang with Comfort's song and she could almost see the encouraging light in Helper's eyes as he watched her. Her loneliness softened and lifted, and soon she was asleep.

The next week Mommy and Daddy came back from vacation and picked up their two daughters and took them home. It was the last time Beauty saw Grandma Mary's house. Aunt Rose got married, and the house was sold. The new couple bought a duplex, one side for their family and the other side to be shared by Grandma Mary and Tatha Rose. Beauty didn't mind not going to Grandma Mary's for two weeks every summer because it just didn't feel right in the new house. There wasn't enough room for a willow tree or vegetables and flowers. There was no church with processions in the new neighborhood, and nowhere for her three special friends to hide. Thatha Rose took a bus to the old neighborhood often. She was very lonely without her old church and her old friends. Grandma Mary missed her garden. She looked tired all the time now. The young girl withdrew into herself even more.

Daddy started taking the whole family on vacations after that. They would all pile into a car and drive a long while, singing "A hundred bottles of beer on the wall," and "Mairsy Dotes." They would stop at roadside picnic tables for lunch and sleep in motels. Mommy had a sore back and couldn't stand camping.

They visited lakes and strange caverns, little old railroad stations with ancient trains that were no longer used, and funny museums in resort towns with tall Victorian houses painted in bright pastels. Daddy took lots and lots of pictures of the family in each place, but mostly of

Mommy. He never seemed to tire of looking at her or photographing her. Sometimes Mommy would complain. "Oh stop, I look awful and I don't need to see photos of myself with my hair such a mess." Daddy would tell her how beautiful she was, and she would smile again, and playfully punch his arm.

There was something very special between them, but they kept it very private, just between themselves. Often Beauty and her sister could feel they just didn't belong in that special feeling. In a strange way that made perfect sense. No one knew about her friends, Comfort, Helper and Shadow, or the marvelous spider. She often wondered when she would see them again, longing for them as the length of time between their visits grew longer and longer.

Sometimes when the family spent a vacation day on a beach by a lake, Beauty was able to wander off on her own for a while. She would always look for a secluded spot and call her friends. Once in a while the three kid friends would come out and they would have a marvelous time. Every time she learned something new in school about a different time in history or a planet revolving around the sun, the foursome would make a great game of it and sail giddily through time and space. They would squeeze their eyes shut, and in a few moments stars were whizzing by as they traveled to another when or a different where. Beauty always held tightly to one of her friends so she wouldn't get lost. She could see the different times and places, but she couldn't find her way there or back. When she learned about St. Francis, they created a wonderful game in which the gentle monk helped her find the elusive wolf.

At the Lake

Sometimes the heart sees what is invisible to the eye.

H. Jackson Brown, Jr.

Morning came and Traveler flew in circles inspecting the land to see if any danger was approaching. There was nothing moving except the small creatures looking for their first meal of the day. Traveler did the same, diving for the water to feed along the banks. Fluffy caught a substantial breakfast in short order, and after feasting the two friends napped in the sunshine near the banks of the stream. They stayed a few days, their sense of adventure dulled by the need for rest. Fluffy asked her friend, "Is Traveler your real Name? Have you had your naming ceremony already?"

"Yes my friend," the goose answered. "It's my real Name." "So, your Spirit Journey is to travel?" asked Fluffy. "Yes, to Travel, here and now and in other places and times." "What does that mean?" asked the confused wolf pup. "You will understand when you have your Naming ceremony", was the reply. Fluffy couldn't hide her impatience at that response. She stretched her neck and snapped her teeth.

On the fourth evening as the stars brilliantly popped into view, they set out to follow the same star that began their journey. Traveler taught Fluffy how to recognize the same star, even though its position had changed somewhat in the last few days. There was a precise movement that happened during the turn of each day. Once you got used to it, knowing where to look became easy as breathing. This was the beginning of Fluffy's education on never being lost. Finding your way by the stars was partly a matter of memorizing the minute daily changes until you could feel it in your bones.

It wasn't really thinking, but it wasn't feeling with the heart either. The sensing simply became an awareness that was a part of your extended being, and it was possible to send your awareness out in all directions around you, gathering information.

Traveler was wise enough to remind Fluffy that this was one of the things mother would have taught her if she had been with her. "This isn't magic, my friend, just part of your true nature as one of the Children of the Earth. Before long you will be guiding me to places I never would have found without you." Fluffy was skeptical. "How is that possible? You already know all there is about finding your way, and even if I catch up with you, I won't be any better."

"It's not about better, it's about specific gifts. I am very, very good at finding my way by the stars and by feel, but only from the air. You will be able to find your way on the ground, which has many places I never see. You have to see things first in order to learn to sense them. Running around on the ground through forests would be a waste of my ability to fly, so there are places I will never learn alone. I'll bet if I teach you what I know from flying in the air and you teach me what you know about what's on the ground, we could be a really great team! We could find anything and we could hide from anything." Traveler was grinning with delight at his own fantasies.

They spent several weeks traveling together, taking many detours from their intention to follow one star, in order to help Fluffy learn navigation. Sometimes they flew, and sometimes in woods and thickets Traveler rode on Fluffy's back or half hopped/half flew in more open spaces. Fluffy loved the forests and soon her sense of smell became part of her ability to navigate. She could tell the north side of a tree from the south side, even in the dark, just by sniffing the bark. She began to realize that every meadow, every hill or patch of trees or body of water had its own "feel". She absorbed it all and before long could call the "feel" of a distant place to her. She found her way by noticing if the feel became weaker or stronger as she walked. Before long she had absorbed enough information so that she knew the feel of every place she must pass through to get to her destination. The star was calling her to a specific place. She knew that now, but didn't understand why. Traveler was astounded at how fast she was learning, and very proud to be her teacher.

The two friends traveled a long way north, moving very fast as they shared between Traveler's flight and Fluffy's easy, loping stride. The star they followed was brighter now, and Fluffy felt a new ....something. A rightness in the journey that she couldn't explain. They stayed close to valleys to keep the trip easy, but more and more mountains brought the horizon nearer. Lakes were much colder than a few days earlier, and rivers rushed with more power than either of them had seen before. One night in sheer ecstasy, Fluffy stood at the edge of a lake and howled at the waxing moon. Then again, and again. Her body felt strong and powerful. Her spirit was free. She had a true friend, a trusted companion. Once again she wondered how she could be as true a friend to Traveler as he was to her. She made up her mind she would not miss any chance that came her way to show her friendship. She hadn't thought about herding sheep in days. She went to sleep content, thinking about the young female people who came into her dreams so often.

She came upon a small lake, partially lit by a half moon, with some strange looking things sticking up high out of the water, and what looked like a floating fence, marking off an area close to a little sand beach. She was surprised and not a little dismayed at the strong scent of People she found all around the lake. Glancing up the hill, she saw structures a lot like the cut grass place but much smaller. Just big enough for a People to stand erect. Faint lights were gleaming from the structures and her keen nose told her the concentration of People was in and around the hilltop.

She bent for long drink of water, certain no one was near by just now. It was alarming when an anguished cry reached her. It came in the language of the heart, carrying such a lonely sadness. She expanded her senses and felt a young, female human walking outdoors near the top of the hill, clearly looking for something or someone. After a few minutes the girl went back inside and Fluffy could feel her despair. It was much like her own, living with the kindly sheep dogs and missing Mother so terribly.

Just as she was about to move on, suddenly the girl appeared at the edge of the forest, near the lake. Fluffy lifted her head from her final drink and sniffed carefully, taking a few steps in her direction. There was something very familiar about this girl. A tentative probe was sent out. Who are you? What is your Name? She felt the girl's surprise and jolt of recognition as she answered, "I don't know. What's yours?

They talked for a few minutes about perhaps helping each other earn the naming ceremony. The sense of familiarity grew stronger as they talked but Fluffy couldn't figure out where it came from. She was about to ask where and when they had met before when the girl reached out to touch her, but suddenly popped out of sight like a puff of smoke. Fluffy felt a blow on her head, just above her eyes, but could see nothing that might have caused it.

~~~~~~~~~~~~~~~~

Finally Beauty graduated from her Brownie troop and became a real Girl Scout. At the first meeting the other new girl was named Roseanne. She smiled at Beauty and before long the two were fast friends. Sleepover friends. Roseanne was a timid girl with a rather plain face, but she had sparkling eyes and an infectious giggle. Her two older twin brothers were mean and picked on her every time their mother wasn't watching. They started in on Beauty during her first overnight visit but she could see they didn't have any real power. She used just a little bit of the silver strands on them, just enough so they lost their balance. After a couple of times they avoided her, looking sideways with uncertain suspicion as she and Roseanne shrugged them off.

Roseanne worshipped Beauty and hung on every word she said. After a while, Beauty got up the courage to ask her if she had any special friends. The answer was, "I think I used to, but I forgot." For the first time since Grandma Mary shushed her, Beauty told another person about her special friends. Her new friend hung on her every word, with big, round eyes and a breathless "Wow" every now and then.

The two of them began creating games with a host of imaginary characters, traveling the known world and outer space as champions and heroines and adored leaders.
~~~~~~~~~~~~~~~~

Basements became dangerous dungeons and swing sets were space ships. Dolls and stuffed toys were their obedient subjects. Secretly Beauty's heart was aching because these really were imaginary characters. She couldn't see or hear any of them the way she could her special friends. She never told Roseanne that none of it was real for her. At least she had a friend to pretend with her.

Summer came and now that they were real Girl Scouts, they could go away to camp without their parents. Mommy drove them to a place in the woods and made sure they had a bed assigned in a bunk house and a spending allowance at the camp store for ice cream and other treats. They had to make their own cots up, and hang their shirts and pants on pegs on the wall. The rest of their clothes were kept under the bunk in a suitcase or duffle bag. Strangest of all were the outhouses; adventuresome but rather smelly.

Each of the bunk houses had a name and two Scout Leaders assigned to it. Their Leaders were Miss Amy and Miss Jen. The two friends were in the bunk house named Wolf Den. They learned the houses would compete for scout badges during the two weeks of the camp.

Beauty was excited by the biggest patch of woods she had ever seen. Miss Jen told her it was called a forest, not just woods. Best of all there was a lake with a dock and diving board and small beach. They would learn about animals and maybe see spiders. Her heart took a great leap at that news. The first night, Roseanne cried a lot, calling "mommy, mommy" over and over.

Breakfast was early and the morning was chilly and foggy. They had oatmeal and hot chocolate, and immediately began their first lesson, which was gathering kindling for the fire that would cook their lunch. Beauty felt more at home than she ever had in her life, and hugged herself in delight. It felt "right" here in the forest. She tried to remember the music from Peter and the Wolf, and when she looked at a forest creature or smelled the pines, a few strains of sound would dance around her. She learned quickly how to find dry kindling and why birch was best for starting a fire. When she was picked to find thicker pieces, big around as her arm, she felt she had passed her first test.

When some of the other girls squealed at the sight of a bug she would pick it up and show them it was safe. She always asked permission of the bug first, but since it was in her special language, no one else knew. If the creature sent a message to leave it alone, she left it alone. When Miss Amy told her to be more careful because some of the bugs weren't safe, she asked for pictures of the dangerous ones so she wouldn't have to reveal the secret language that already taught her. She got a badge for learning about forest bugs.

The days slipped by quickly. One day there was mail call at lunch time. Almost everyone had a letter from home. Roseanne had been unhappy and crying every day, and when she opened her mom's note, she howled with homesickness. Nothing would comfort her and she wouldn't play. If a Scout leader forced her to try, she would throw up. She was so sad she didn't even want to talk to her only friend. A few more days passed and Beauty was obviously the only one who didn't get a letter from her mom. Some kids had even gotten packages with cookies or gum or some special treat. One of the girls began to taunt Beauty about being an orphan because no one cared about her enough to send a letter.

Beauty stuck her chin in the air and threw herself into camp activities. She took swimming lessons and beginning archery, which she loved, and went on hikes where she learned about telling direction by moss on trees, and things that were safe to pick and eat. Miss Jen handed her a green twig and said, “here, chew on this”, and she giggled in surprise as her mouth filled with the delightful taste of root beer.

One night the sadness came rushing in and she called her guardian angel to come talk to her. Nothing happened. She snuck out into the forest, calling her special friends to come out. No one came. She got caught coming back in and said she needed to use the outhouse. She was scolded for going alone at night and promised not to do it again. She crawled under the rough, wool blanket and fell asleep with hot tears on her cheeks.

She found herself at the edge of the forest, near the lake. There was half a moon so she could see pretty well. A dark shape was drinking water from the lake. She held her breath, nearly motionless. It was the biggest creature she had seen so far in the wonderful forest. It raised its head and turned, sniffing carefully as it took a few steps in her direction. At first she thought it must be somebody’s large dog, wandering into the forest alone. That was pretty scary.

Then it hit her with a jolt; this was Wolf! But it was different. There was no hungry grin with yellow teeth dripping saliva. The eyes were warm brown, not red rimmed at all. She remembered wolf changing in her dreams when she was younger, and was glad to see this was still how it looked. She felt a tentative probe touch her that left a warm feeling. Then the probe reached into her mind. “Who are you? What is your Name?”

Beauty couldn’t have been more stunned. She hadn’t talked about Name with anyone since the last time she and her friend the spider had been together. She sent out her soundless answer. “I don’t know yet. What is yours?”

Wolf studied her for a few moments. “I don’t know either. I haven’t had my naming ceremony. Maybe we can help each other.” Beauty nearly popped with joy. A new special friend! One who spoke her special language! Once again she wasn’t alone.

She reached out her arms and launched herself toward the wolf for a hug.... and cracked her head soundly on the floor as she fell out of bed. Miss Amy bolted toward her, swooping her up and carrying her to the nurse. The nurse put ice on the growing lump on her forehead. (Right in the middle, wouldn’t you know!) It was determined she would be fine and she was tucked back in her bed. She hugged herself happily. She remembered the cover on the record with the frightening wolf picture. She remembered loving the forest story it had told with music. She knew this wasn’t just a dream. It was part of her Spirit Journey.

Then camp was over and Roseanne’s mother came to bring the girls home. Roseanne threw herself at her mother, hanging on with arms and legs as though afraid she would leave. She had never gotten over her homesickness in spite of daily letters. Beauty sighed, and her lip trembled but she refused to cry, and thought about Wolf instead. When she was dropped off at home, mommy was waiting, reaching out for a hug. The taunting about being an orphan and no one caring enough to write her a letter at camp rose up fiercely. Beauty trembled with anger, crossed her arms, and stomped off to her room without a word. The distance between them grew again.

One Christmas when she was in third grade there was a box under the tree with her name on it. She tried to lift it and shake it, but it was too heavy. It was too small for the bike she wanted, and too big for anything else she could imagine. It tantalized her for days, but when Christmas Eve came and it was time to open gifts, she tore into the package only to have her excitement turn into disappointment. “A box of books! Who wants a box of books?” She said “thank you” very politely and tried not to sulk.

The next day after church and the family Christmas dinner, there was nothing to do, so she picked up one of the books and went grumpily to her bedroom to read it. The cover of the book read, “Black Beauty” and by the time she reached the third page, she was living the story as if it was her own. Bed time came, and she was told to put down the book until tomorrow and turn off her light. She waited till the house was quiet, then snuck into the bathroom and closed the door before turning on the light. She finished the book that night, then took it to bed with her, playing with the story in her imagination until she fell asleep.

The box was now a chest of treasures. “Little Women” and “The Five Penneys” and all the children’s classics captured her heart and set her imagination on fire. When she had finished every one and asked for more, Mommy took her to the library and got her a card. She read and read and read. Three books every week and when summer came, five books every week. She forgot her loneliness when she was reading, fully entering the adventure of each story. After a while, she began making stories with her own mind that were as much fun as reading.

Oddly, the more she read and made up stories, the more her angel and the three special friends faded away.

But she never forgot the processions in the Chicago streets with Grandma Mary, and helping the priest weave shining spirit strands among the people. She never forgot the dream with the wolf who had no name. Her family all went to church every Sunday, but she only saw someone weaving spirit strands once in a while. None of them could do it as well as that first priest, and she knew her weaving was also better than any of these. Much better. But she was frightened of being caught helping to weave the strands and having to face the big darkness, so she just watched and waited. Maybe when she learned her true name, she would be stronger. Maybe then her three friends would come back again, and the angel would visit her at night. Maybe even the great spider, but she had learned a bit and knew the spider was probably no longer alive.

~~~~~~~~~~~~~~~~

It had been a glorious winter day. Beauty had gotten a sled and ice skates for Christmas and was discovering the thrill of balance and speed. Early that Saturday morning, Daddy and her uncle and all five kids went to the big hill at the park and rode their sleds down over and over. The men helped the other kids get their sleds back up the hill, but she was the only one who went all the way to the top by herself and came flying down; sometimes sitting and steering with her feet, and sometimes flat on her tummy, steering with her hands, sometimes losing control and tumbling. It was such fun she squealed and screamed as she raced downhill. Daddy laughed a lot, and even her uncle, who was usually not much fun, couldn't help grinning. They played until icy fingers started to stiffen and hunger drove them home to hot soup and grilled cheese sandwiches.

That night after dinner, Daddy said, "Come with me. I have something to show you." They went back to the park, this time to the frozen pond. Some people had built a bonfire near the edge, and there was someone selling hot chocolate. Daddy opened a canvas bag and took out her skates and a pair for himself. That night under the park lights he taught her to skate, and it was the most wonderful night of her life. He held her hands and skated backwards as he taught her how to move her feet and bend her knees. Soon they were skating side by side, and he taught her
~~~~~~~~~~~~~~~~

how to stop very quickly. Once she mastered that, he taught her how to stop very gracefully, with an arching turn of her body.

They rested by the bonfire for a while and he bought them both a steaming hot chocolate. He checked the ties on both their skates and explained the difference between his racing skates and her figure skates. "Please, Daddy, I want to see you race," she begged. He got up and sped around the pond so fast she gasped, brought her hands to her mouth and thought he must be an angel or be a famous star or something. They skated together again for a while, then when she began to shiver, headed home in the car. The trip home was only a few minutes, but she could hardly stay awake. "My daddy is the best in the world," she thought, as she fell in love for the first time in her life, and hugged herself as though to pull the feeling in closer.

She curled up under her quilt thinking her daddy was as wonderful as her three special friends. She counted off the magical moments of the day in her mind and the only thing that could have made it more perfect would be to share it with her friends. She wished she could talk to Spider about daddy and skating and the thrill of flying on a sled, then wondered if the wolf had a mommy and daddy. She imagined sliding on a rainbow, gathering stardust in her hands and throwing it overhead. As the sparkling bits fell around her, catching in her hair and eyelashes, sleep took over.

In the Cave

Lead me from the unreal to the real.
Lead me from darkness to light.
Lead me from death to immortality.

The Upanishads

She woke up by a small river, with a barren, dry hill rising next to it. "What a strange place," thought Beauty. "That hill is just rocks and dirt. How can anything live here?" A wisp of smoke was curling out of the top of the hill and it seemed to call to her. She began walking up the slope, sensing an aliveness similar to what she felt in a forest. "Comfort. Shadow. Helper. Can you hear me?" She waited, then sighed her sadness when no answer came.

A rhythmic, thrumming noise was coming from inside the hill and curiosity kept her climbing upward. She came to a small, partially hidden entrance and the rhythmic noise grew louder. Cautiously edging inside, she kept her back against the cave wall and looked around. A wolf was in the midst of dancing figures. The figures were nearly translucent and she rubbed her eyes, expecting them to disappear, but they kept dancing. She listened intently to the rhythm, allowing it to enter her body. The notes of a flute rippled in her throat feeling like a song she wanted to sing. The dancers looked more solid and the wolf let out a howl; not a mournful sound, but one of great power that thrilled her to her core.

She was so entranced she didn't notice the great Orb Weaver above her head, weaving shining strands into the stories of the children of the earth or the ancient one in the red blanket. Every other being faded from her notice, until only one remained. The wolf turned to her, wrapping her in warm welcome with its sweet essence. She reached out to touch one silky ear, suddenly overwhelmed with a feeling of "forever". The wolf spoke, not in words but deep inside her. "I will call you. Listen for me. You don't have to be alone."

Beauty came awake in her bed on a cold winter morning. "Oh no!" Squeezing her eyes shut, she cried with all her being, "Please don't leave me. Come back. How will I ever find you? I'm calling you now. Please, come back!" There was only silence.

~~~~~~~~~~~~~~~~

They woke in the morning and the dream of the girl was driven from Fluffy's mind by the beauty of their surroundings. They were amazed to see that their lake was just a small cove off a larger body of water. The cove was ringed with tall pine trees. Very tall. Tall enough to surprise them both. At the top of many of them perched large, rather flat, bowl shaped nests. As they watched, a flurry of eagles dove toward the water, grabbed fish in their talons, and returned to their nests to feed themselves and their young. Every few minutes some of them would dive, fish and return.

The power and precision were magnificent to watch. Traveler and Fluffy were thrilled at the sight, and a spontaneous wave of excitement and delight pulsed from their hearts. After a while the feeding ended and the small
~~~~~~~~~~~~~~~~

cove became peaceful, giving over to smaller birds looking for seed and scratching on the ground.

Traveler entered the water, seeking his breakfast but being careful to stay near the bank, hidden in the reeds, doing his best not to look like a fish. Fluffy walked into the pine forest, sniffing her way carefully as the ground sloped upward more and more steeply. Food was easy to find and she was quickly satisfied. She began exploring in earnest, letting the feeling of this place seep into her and settle in her bones.

It was a good place to be. A rocky clearing opened in the pines, and on top of a tall ledge there sat an eagle. It cocked its head and examined Fluffy carefully. Fluffy's heart leapt in an enthusiastic greeting, and the eagle seemed to grin. "Easy young lady, you are too quick to expose yourself. I could be a rogue and very dangerous." Fluffy gave her best version of a grin right back. "I don't think so. Your heart feels so good I learned your language almost instantly; or, did you learn mine?"

"There are many wolves in the world. I learned your language long ago, so this time the congratulations belong to you for being a quick learner. Now pay attention to your first lesson. Some eagles are rogues and not all wolves have a good heart. Use more caution if you wish to live long." The lesson was almost lost on Fluffy as a wild idea captured her. "You know other wolves?" she asked the eagle. "Do you know Mother and my brother Fuzz Ball? Can you help me find them? I can't remember Mother's scent any more. Will she know me? Will she want me? I'm getting pretty good in the woods and I wouldn't be much trouble. Do you know Mother?"

"Easy, easy," said the eagle. "So many questions. My goodness! You come from a direction I've never traveled. I doubt if I know your mother, but I know something about you. You have far to travel and much to learn before you can keep the promise of your name." "Do you know my true name?" asked Fluffy in a voice so excited she nearly yipped like a pup. "Will you tell me? Can I have my naming ceremony now?" "Most certainly not," huffed the eagle. You have much to learn first. Now, will you be quiet and listen for a change?

"OK," said Fluffy, "but can my friend Traveler listen with me? He's just down the hill. He's my best friend and we go everywhere together and he taught me how to find my way and hunt for food and he saved my life….." "HUSH!" snapped the eagle. "Call him up here, then sit down and shut up! Don't you know anything about silence? Of course not. Silly of me. So, that's our first lesson. You will learn silence, starting right now." "But…" "HUSH. NOW!"

Traveler swooped overhead, dived for a bush, and tucked his head under one wing for a nap. When Fluffy tried to speak to him, the eagle flapped its wings in indignation and stared her down. Fluffy sat, silent. The day wore on. The eagle flew in and out of the clearing, checking on her silence. Traveler slept on. Fluffy sat. She scratched. She cleaned a paw. She gnawed lightly on her old burn scar. Every time she started to drift toward sleep, the eagle flapped by within inches of her face. So, OK, no sleeping. Silence.

Fluffy's body began to relax, almost as though she was falling asleep, but different somehow. She was exquisitely alert. She noticed grains of dirt sparkling in the sunlight. She became aware of a low hum all around her. Insects, many, many insects in a stunning variety were on the ground, in the ground, in the bushes and grasses, on the ledge, flying and hopping. She could feel the pulse of their life force. It was not like a language she could learn, but she got a clear message from the hum; "all is well".

She relaxed even more and became aware of a thin, whispery sound. Sap, flowing through branches, pulsing into leaves on bushes and trees, whispered with purpose. Fluffy wasn't sure what their purpose was, but she was absolutely certain they knew. Tiny molecules of something, green stuff? came alive and changed form as they spread themselves through the veins of leaves and gathered the energy of the sun. Life poured out of them and filled the air. The insects danced. Fluffy's heart was joyful.

The sound of the tiniest twig snapping rang out like a shot, and she became aware of a big cat nearby. She "felt" the powerful animal and found the sleepiness of a full belly. The cat walked up the ledge to the other side for a long nap in the sun. Fluffy's senses followed part way up the ledge and she became aware of the finest movement. Amazingly slight, but movement. The rock was alive! Everything was alive! She was shocked out of her reverie, and she felt the eagle coming before it was in sight, and sent out a silent greeting. The eagle landed on a nearby bit of ledge. "You learn quickly" it said softly. "Welcome to our home. I am going to enjoy teaching you."

Eagle said the most important lesson was that absolutely everything, everywhere has a voice. Some could only communicate a sense or a feeling, and others could clearly share ideas, but all voices are important. Eagle then said something completely unintelligible to Fluffy, in a very loud and passionate voice. When Fluffy strained to understand, she caught a feeling from Eagle that her efforts were rejected. She wasn't worthy of attention. It was an awful feeling and she wanted to slink away and hide.

"Fluffy", said Eagle softly. "Pay close attention. What you are feeling right now is how others will feel if you reject them because their voice is different than yours.

You need to be cautious and make sure their hearts are open, but never reject a voice just because it's different. You might lose your most important ally, and worse, you will harm your own soul by causing another pain. Now relax, I didn't mean you are worthless. It was just part of the lesson." Fluffy determined to never cause that kind of pain, and was even more attentive in the listening lessons.

The next morning Fluffy got on Traveler's back and they flew with Eagle. He found what he wanted, and landed in a secluded place where they could observe without being seen. It was a human man with a dog. Fluffy felt for their hearts as she was instructed, and felt a cold wall from both of them. She withdrew her probe and looked to Eagle. "These two do not have the language of the heart," said the eagle. "Not the male people nor the dog. It is best to avoid their notice if you can, but you can still get a sense of how dangerous they are, if at all. Don't try to touch them with your heart, just listen, very lightly, and don't reveal yourself if you can help it."

The man had no voice at all and felt hard and lifeless, but the dog exuded brutality; an urge to tear something apart. Anything at all. Fluffy was quivering with shock and fought the urge to run. Eagle spoke softly. "Always check the heart, and then listen for the feeling before revealing yourself. Some who don't have the language of the heart are harmless, but some are very dangerous. Let's go, quickly."

The next morning Eagle said, "lets have another trip. I think you will like this one a lot better. Traveler, you fly with me, and Fluffy you see if you can follow us by sensing where we are. Send your awareness into the places we are looking down at as we fly, and come along. I promise no tricks. I just want to see how good you are at finding your way."

The two birds flew off and Fluffy settled happily into the energy of "finding", allowing her essence to feel after them. It was very easy because they were backtracking the way Fluffy and Traveler had come just days ago. Around sunset she lost the "feel" so she stopped for food and water, then laid down near a warm rock to listen and rest. In the morning she awoke, aware she was to cross the hill that lined the curving river, and there would be another body of water on the other side. She loped along, refreshed, attentive now to listening as well as sensing and feeling, as miles dropped easily behind her. The whispers and hum of life were growing more familiar and again she felt joy at being part of it.

She topped the treeless hill, and looked down at a winding river which was nearly hidden by the trees and brush on its banks. The valley was teeming with life. She nearly bolted for the river, but caught herself and searched carefully with her heart and her senses. She could feel the pulse of many kinds of life, but no danger or cold, hard places. Looking across the valley to the next hill, she could see it was even more barren, and knew she was on the edge of a very different place.

Her eye caught two small specks on a hilltop across the way, and a cautious probe revealed Traveler and Eagle. She started to run toward them, but again caught herself as she noticed a thick curl of smoke coming from a spot near the river. She couldn't see past the trees, so she checked it out with her heart and was startled to hear a loud chuckle. "Aha, you are here, finally. Long I have waited for you, young one." The heart reaching toward her was wide open and totally peaceful. She glanced up looking for Traveler and Eagle, but they had left their perch. As she cautiously moved toward the voice, she listened very carefully to everything around her. All voices seemed to agree that this was a good place. The very earth had a feeling of waiting aliveness. She came to a green wall of bushes and trees, welcoming her with soft whispers.

Fluffy pushed her way through and found herself facing an old man with weathered, brown skin and a smoldering pipe, its smoke blending with the heavier smoke from the fire he was tending. “Welcome. Your heart really is as good as I hoped,” said the old one. “You are a People,” said the startled wolf. “How is it you know the language of the heart and can speak with me?” Traveler and Eagle had landed nearby, and Traveler was as stunned as Fluffy at finding a People with an open heart. “Yes, please tell us,” urged Traveler. “I have just spent weeks training this pup to avoid all people because they are dangerous and don’t have the language. Who are you? What’s happening here?”

Eagle flapped his wings and landed lightly on the old man’s shoulder. “Let me introduce you to this wise one who has been adopted by the wolf clan. We call him Teacher. He has brought wisdom and knowledge to many of us, and he has been waiting for you two. He is here to teach you about the People. Traveler, you will be mating soon, and it’s time for you to learn this so you can pass it on to your family. Fluffy, you must learn from Teacher if you wish to get closer to having your naming ceremony.” The old man grinned at the eagle. “Good job, Messenger. You have brought them here and you have told them why. You make my job much easier.”

Fluffy stared at the eagle. “Your name is Messenger? Your real name? You have promised to carry messages? Can you find my Mother? Can you tell her where I am and that I miss her? Can you tell her I’m doing my best to be a real wolf? Can you visit mum and dad and tell them I’m fine, just looking for my naming ceremony. They are sheep dogs, but they will understand. Can you....”

"Hold it, hold it," said the old man. "Slow down and listen." "She does that," said Messenger." "Yup," said Traveler. "She launches into a whirlwind of questions and she doesn't start with the easy ones." Fluffy sighed and flopped down, her chin on her front paws. "No answers again," she thought with sad resignation. The old man looked at Fluffy with compassion. It reminded her of the first day mum and dad found her, and she relaxed.

"Young one, I don't know if your Mother is still alive or if you will ever find her, but I do know this. You are a real wolf, a fine one in fact, and you will find the answers to your most important questions yourself. When you learn to find your own answers, you will be able to help other children of the earth do the same, and that is a very good and useful thing to do." With that the old man stood up and invited everyone to explore the hillside for a good cave. They needed one for tomorrow's ceremony.

Fluffy didn't miss a beat. "Is it my naming ceremony?" she began breathlessly. "Is it…." "Hush!" said Messenger, before she could launch another string of passionate pleas for information. "No more questions now, let's just find a cave."

The small party crossed the river and began exploring the nearly barren hillsides. They were pocked here and there with shallow caves. One housed a nest of rattle snakes, and the other explorers held back as Fluffy practiced listening and feeling. "Sleep," said Fluffy. "This is their sleep time, and we should leave them alone." Messenger grinned and nodded. They kept looking and at the top of one low hill they came upon a hole in the ground. There was a draft of cool air rising from the hole. "This is it," said Teacher. "This is the top vent for a very large cave. We will find the main entrance somewhere down the hill. They separated to search the hill more quickly, and before long Teacher called out, and they all followed his call to an opening that was partly hidden by a large boulder.

This time, they all worked together, each of them sending their awareness into the cave, sensing and listening for anything that might be in there. It was utterly silent; not even the hum of insects came from the cave. They entered and once their eyes adjusted to dimness, they could see because of the light coming from the hole at the top. There were drawings on the walls. Shapes etched in black and red, resembling people and animals and insects. A sliver of moon pointed toward a cascade of stars, all etched in white. A yellow sun sent rays into the earth and sprung back out as corn. Teacher told them they were looking at the story of an ancient race, and the better they learned to understand its message, the better each of them would be at living their purpose. They all fell silent for some time, examining the glyphs in awe.

Back outside, Teacher began to gather wood and carry it into the cave. He had to walk down nearly to the river to find it, then bring it back up hill. "Wait," cried Traveler. "I can help. Tie a pile on my back and I'll fly it up the hill for you. It will be much faster." Teacher looked doubtful until Fluffy explained that carrying things much larger than himself was part of Traveler's magic. The work went quickly after that. As the pile grew and grew, Fluffy asked how big a fire they were going to build in the cave. "A very small one," replied Teacher. "But it must last a long time."

As evening came, they all went to the river for a last drink of water and filed into the cave where Teacher built a fire. The smell brought the old fear of fire back up for Fluffy, but she reminded herself she was with magical friends and she would be perfectly safe. Of course she would.

Teacher had brought a drum into the cave with him. “Fluffy, I am called Teacher, but the knowledge I carry is not now part of the world you are used to. I will drum us into a Dream Time. If you pay attention, you can learn many things, perhaps even something of your destiny. Traveler, your purpose is to carry people in many dimensions. Will you lead our journey please?” Traveler bowed, all sense of joking silenced.

The drum began softly. All of them slipped into the Silence Fluffy had learned the day before. Traveler began to move around the fire, his wings lifting and dropping, opening and closing with the drumbeat. The fire flickered and the drawings on the cave walls seemed to come alive. The people danced, the animals and insects began to move, the soft sshhhing sound of corn growing joined the drumming. One star, the farthest one from the moon, pulsed with white light. The rhythmic thrum, thrum, thrum brought all the sounds of the Silence into harmony, as though all the earth and those on it were pulsing with the same beat. Teacher got up with his drum and joined the dance, and the rest followed.

An ancient dancer raised a flute and its sound swirled around the drumming. They danced and danced, taking turns feeding the fire. One by one the figures left the walls and joined the dance, until the great cave was filled with sound and motion. The last person to leave the wall was withered and ancient, but danced with more passion and energy than anyone else; long, white hair flying with the spinning and leaping. There was a huge, orb weaver spider sitting on the bright blanket the old one wore.

The last notes of the flute slipped away, the drumbeat slowed and softened, and all the dancers gathered to sit around the fire. Traveler stopped last, bowing before the old one then settling next to Fluffy in rapt attention. Teacher spoke first. “It has been many long seasons since we last met, holy one. I have remembered what you taught me in my youth. The generation you told me to watch for are beginning to arrive. Are you here to teach again?"

The sounds of Silence compressed and closed in until it became difficult to tell the difference between seeing and hearing or feeling. The great orb weaver leaped to the top of the cave, then spun a shining strand, crossing back and forth above the watchers and weaving a huge web. The shining web reflected the firelight, and everyone could see/hear/feel its message. It was the story of all the children of the earth; all of them, everywhere and everywhen. Beauty and joy. Terror and conflict. Kindness and intelligence. Cruelty and stupidity. Sweetness and foolishness. Love and hate. Cooperation and manipulation. Every possible choice and experience in all the generations of the earth was contained in the Orb Weaver's web of life.

The last image was of a young, female People, dark haired and dark eyed, walking a lonely road and searching. Fluffy's heart leaped in recognition, compassion filling her at the lonely sadness in the dark eyes. Traveler was trembling. Fluffy was both delighted and horrified. The rest seemed to know already, and they began a soft chant, keeping time with the barely beating drum.

The ancient one finally spoke, in a voice as dry and raspy as old leaves. "Life on this planet is coming to another crossroad. It will be once again a time of choice between all you have witnessed. This is a planet of duality. Light and dark belong in a dance in which both have a valued place, but sometimes they get out of balance. It is in bringing them back into balance that the children of the earth learn and grow. Right here and right now, darkness prevails. Very few humans or animals know the language of the heart. They walk a path of forgetting that leads to loneliness and fear and finally despair. Once in every many thousands of years life shrugs, and only those who know the language of the heart and the sound of Silence survive on this earth, and the light comes back. This is such a time."

Piercing, black eyes bored into Fluffy and Traveler and Messenger and Teacher. The raspy voice resumed. "Your names tell you your mission. You all have great work to do. Traveler, never underestimate the power of your name. Never underestimate how far or how fast you can travel, or how many you can lead or carry with you. Teacher, your bones are getting old and creaky, but many more are coming to learn. Keep sending smoke signals with your pipe so they can find you. Messenger, you must fly farther to deliver the call to others and lead the right ones to Teacher. You, young wolf, have one more thing to do, to discover your name. These three will help you, but be sure to take care of Teacher. He must survive."

The drumming suddenly halted, and the only evidence of the ancient dancers were the painted glyphs on the cave walls. The four friends sat alone around the fire. Teacher spoke after a few moments. "Right now, Fluffy, if you're ready, let's begin your first lesson. Traveler, this is for you too. Fluffy, you discovered there is more to reality than your eyes see the first time you hopped on Traveler's back to fly with him. In fact, physical reality is not solid at all. That's why you could hear the rocks and trees. The universe is a great swirl of energy, constantly shifting, moving and creating. There is no limit to the scope of sound and color and physical formations it can take. There is no place where life is not, and no such thing as good or bad, just formations created by life's thought."

"Here on this earth, the energy patterns and thought forms are very specific to creating the experience of balance. There is a cyclical pattern of things being out of balance followed by those who work to restore balance.

That is a work, a purpose if you will, assigned to all the children of the earth, no matter what form they are in. Each has a part to play. Within this greater purpose, each individual has a personal purpose, and so the great tapestry of life is woven. Some call it the web of life."

"My purpose is to teach this to as many as possible, and your purpose is to do what you are called to do in order for others to have the chance to learn so they can become part of restoring balance. For all of us, our greatest joy and fulfillment comes from living our Purpose. Some call it a great Spirit Journey, because we work in all the dimensions of reality, not just the physical. Traveler, do you understand part of your purpose is to carry people to their teachers?" The great goose nodded, an intent expression on his face.

"We are at a place in the cycle in which the balance is tipped very far toward what we call 'the dark.' There is not much time left to restore balance. If we fail, the experiment called Earth will end, and all the energy will return to Source for recycling. There are some children of the earth who are awakening to this knowledge. They are searching for their Teachers and they will need protecting." Fluffy burst into questions. "Why do they need protecting? Who would hurt them if they're doing something good for all of us? How are we supposed to know who they are so we can help? How much time do we have? I don't understand; what is light and what is dark?"

Traveler shook his head and rolled his eyes. Messenger flapped his wings and said, "SILENCE". Fluffy looked worried but stopped asking. Teacher chuckled and continued. "Light and dark are spectrums of color and sound within the energy of all that is. Both include vast potential and are meant to work together. On this earth, if dark becomes too strong, fear and anger and a cold-heartedness take over. The children of the earth become self centered and often violent. Enough violence will destroy the earth."

"If, on the other hand, light becomes too strong, the children of the earth bliss out, forget the learning life is seeking here, and skip off the planet on a sunbeam. Too much light and there is no reason for this dimension of time and space to exist. The earth would cease to exist. Everything is expanding or contracting. It is in finding balance that Life gains knowledge of itself and its potential grows."

"There are also many, many children of the earth who are asleep to all of this. They believe forms are solid and time is linear and the same rules apply to everyone, all the time. Some are kind and some are not. Most of them are fearful, even when they pretend not to be. They simply can't imagine not having a body, or expanding their awareness through time and space, and that's mostly what makes them fearful, and unfortunately, unpredictable. They are easily swayed by the most powerful force, either dark or light, that happens to catch their attention. I must give you one very grave warning here. If you use your powers and your purpose to deceive and manipulate those who are asleep, even for what appears to be a good cause, you will harm your own soul. You may guide them or inspire them using truth and honesty, but if they refuse to follow, simply walk away."

"The dark side is very strong right now as I said, and we don't have much time. Be very careful to avoid anyone who walks in the dark. If they can feel your light, they will do their best to kill you. They can take any form among the children of the earth, and some of them are able to extend their energy and use it for harm. They are particularly good at this when they are working as a group and are aware of what they are doing and agree on a target. Be very careful to shield yourself from them as much as possible. Meanwhile, you are to find the children of the earth who can be taught to walk in the balance of light and dark and band together for the time of reckoning, when equilibrium must be restored."

"The good news I have for you today is that one is coming who can show you how to use the language of the heart to stop the attack of darkness. She will teach you how to shield your visibility and how to use more wisdom. I don't know when she will arrive, but Messenger spotted her from a treetop the other day, laying in the sun and listening to the voices of the earth. She is almost ready. Meanwhile, we have to take a trip. You start out and I'll walk and catch up with you."

Rejection

Our bones are dry, our hope has gone; we are done for.

Ezekiel 37:11

Just before the fifth grade the family moved to a new town. Beauty had a baby brother now, and he was lots of fun. He didn't know the special language, but he was happy, and sometimes she would catch him with the kind of look that said he was listening to something no one else could hear.

That Christmas, her Uncle Ernie gave her a book about the Middle Ages and Geoffrey Chaucer. Someone else gave her Robin Hood and another relative gave her a scrapbook collection filled with years of cut out Sunday comics about Prince Valiant.

Her heart exploded with romance and her mind leapt into creating stories where she wore heavy, long gowns and inspired brave young men to glorious action. When there was a tragedy, and there always had to be one, she would imagine herself kneeling in a bare room with her head bowed and covered. Sometimes her stories felt like stories, and sometimes like remembering. Once in a great while the wolf would be watching her from a distance. She hated the distance, but felt comforted anyway.

Sister Mary Agnes taught seventh grade algebra and English composition at Beauty's school. If you were taking college prep classes, you had her for English and Algebra two years in a row. Everyone was afraid of Sister Mary Agnes. She never smiled, and everyone said it was very hard to get a good grade in her classes. She didn't rap knuckles with a ruler like some of the other teachers, but she gave detentions and long extra homework assignments if you were caught whispering or chewing gum in her class. She caught every mistake and did not mince words telling you about it. If you misspelled a word, you would have to write it on the blackboard 100 times. Her classes were hard.

Algebra was easy for Beauty. She didn't like it much, but she learned the formulas quickly. She had learned how to hide what she was really thinking and feeling very well, and to escape notice by making as few mistakes as possible. She never got into trouble and was a star student. She was called "teachers pet" and had few friends, but she was used to that.

One day Sister Mary Agnes gave the class an assignment to write a short story. It had to be neatly handwritten on two pages of the lined paper everyone used. For Beauty, stories were understood with her special language, so that's what she used to write her assignment. She used her heart to feel the story in her special language, then did her best to put it into people words. That part was hard. She wrote about meeting her friend Spider and learning that it was important for the children of the earth to respect each other. She was careful to leave out the kind of details that her wisdom told her would be misunderstood. Writing the story was fun! It was almost as much fun as reading her favorite books.

Sister Mary Agnes called her in during recess, and Beauty went with her heart in her throat, wondering what awful transgression she had committed. She was smiling! Sister Mary Agnes was actually smiling! The Sister told her she had a wonderful imagination and if she became really good at English she could be an author one day. She might even write books like Black Beauty or even more grown up books. She told her there would be extra credit for any short story or essay she wrote for this class, and Sister Mary Agnes would teach her how to make each one better. Beauty was stunned by the approval. She wasn't used to being praised. She was used to hearing things like, "that's nice honey, but if you had just tried harder it could have been so much better."

Beauty told the Sister she would write for extra credit. Sister Mary Agnes nodded in satisfaction, smiled once more, then the stern look returned as she admonished the girl not to let her regular homework slip. By the time Beauty had done two extra credit papers and went over them with her mentor, she was no longer afraid of the Sister and they were becoming friends. She didn't tell a soul. If anyone found out that she and the stern Sister Mary Agnes were friends, Beauty would really be ridiculed by her peers. She had watched them taunt some unpopular kids and more than anything she wanted to avoid their notice.

That spring, during Lent, she had been sent to church by Mommy to go to confession so she would be ready for Easter. She stayed after confession, and walked alone around the church, saying the required prayers at each of the Stations of the Cross. She liked the ritual of doing this because it reminded her of how she felt during the processions in Chicago when she was little. She particularly related to Jesus and how nobody could see him as he really was. The ridicule she endured was nothing compared to what he suffered! Her heart filled with sadness and love for him.

The circle of light painted around his head reminded her of weaving shining strands, and suddenly an idea struck her. The priests who could weave the strands didn't appear to get attacked by the big darkness. They must know something, or have special protection as priests. An idea flashed with total rightness into her mind. She remembered that during the processions in earlier summers, she thought about being a priest. Suddenly she knew with absolute certainty that she must become a priest. She was flooded with longing to use her special language freely and to weave shining strands together. It felt more "right" than anything she had ever done; even more "right" than writing stories and essays.

She had never seen the Monsignor who was head of the parish do the weaving, but his younger assistant, Father Mike did every once in a while. Beauty asked for an appointment to see him and he welcomed her kindly. She began to talk, and like water spilling through a breaking dam, her story poured out with no details held back. She spoke about her special language and what Spider had taught her. She told him about the processions in Chicago and how when she helped the priest weave the shining strands of spirit she was attacked. With all her heart she wanted to learn how to use her special language and weave the strands and still stay safe. Would he help her become a priest?

Father Mike's eyes were wide and full of shock. His voice was very stern as he spoke. "Beauty, what you are saying is blasphemy. There is no such thing as a "special language". If you speak in a strange language, that's the devil possessing you. What's more, you are human and you don't have a light like Jesus. Worst of all you are committing the sin of Pride by thinking you can be a priest. You are a female and God does not want females as priests. It would be an abomination. Now get out of here and don't ever let me hear you talking this way again. Go to confession, right away, and ask forgiveness for lying and for your sin of Pride. Get out!"

Beauty's whole body was rigid. She felt like a piece of wood as she fled the priest's office. She heard over and over again, "God does not want you because you're a girl." She raced home and threw herself across her bed. She couldn't think. She couldn't feel anything except this stiff woodenness. For days she walked around with her head pounding the awful words and her heart cracking. "God does not want you!"

Then she woke up one morning and the wooden feeling was gone. She was filled with a burning anger. God didn't want her. Her parents and family told her everyone would call her a liar if she kept letting her imagination run away with her. She only had one or two friends, and they didn't want to hear any "weird stuff" from her. She hadn't seen Spider or her special friends in forever. Even the angel had stopped coming a long time ago. Her last hope, the wolf with no Name, had only visited her a few times in dreams. Fine! She didn't need any of them. She would live her life her way and none of them mattered at all. What use was a God who didn't want her? She was free now from all of them, and she stood erect, lifted her chin and walked back into her daily life determined to do exactly as she pleased. A cold, hard shell, like refrigerated steel, formed around her. It was quite comfortable.

That night, Beauty dreamed of the wolf. It was big and dark, with red rimmed eyes and shining yellow teeth that were dripping saliva. It wore a hungry grin. She woke up shaking and sweating, then she put the wolf outside the steely shell like everyone else. No one comes in. The dreams stopped. She was twelve years old. Life was different now. Everything had changed.

Teacher hauled himself off the ground again, wincing as he brushed away twigs and grass. The cuts and bruises would be painful for a while, but he was not seriously hurt. "Fluffy, thank you, you were just in time," said Teacher. "A few more minutes and he would have had that knife at my throat and finished me off." Gagging at the taste of death in her mouth, Fluffy ran off looking for water. When she returned, her friends were sitting in a circle waiting for her.

"What happened? We started with a destination we could all see. Are we in the wrong place? How did they trap you? Couldn't you feel their cruel life force and avoid them? Didn't any of you probe to see if the area was safe? Shouldn't we get out of here? What if there are more of them? The female might bring back others like them. Shouldn't we go? Where should we go? Teacher are you sure you're not badly hurt?" Her friends chuckled at the familiar barrage of questions, then Teacher answered her.

"Beautiful wolf, we are in the right place. We were not trapped, we simply stepped into destiny. I told you as we left the cave of dancing that you had one more thing to do to earn your naming ceremony. You have just done it." "What? You mean kill that man?" asked a stunned Fluffy. "Saving my life," replied teacher. "At some great risk to your own, I might add. The task you had to accomplish was to save a human life." Fluffy's heart thudded. "Do you mean you risked your life so I could save you and earn my naming?" "Well, not exactly," said the sheepish looking man. "I thought there would be someone else you would save, and I would just be there to help. I stuffed my pockets with ashes from our dancing fire because I had an insight someone would have to be blinded for a few seconds. It was a surprise to find my own neck on the line."

"No kidding," chimed in Traveler. "We remembered the ancient one telling us we must keep Teacher alive at all costs and this was really scary. Messenger and I were frantically trying to come up with a plan when we felt you approach. We both realized then that this is why we came to this place. We were here to help while you fulfilled your task. You saved Teacher's life and helped rid the earth of two evil creatures." "Killing felt awful," shuddered Fluffy. "I'm glad you are safe, Teacher, but I feel soiled by ending that man's life."

Teacher responded with great compassion. "It is good you feel that way. It means your heart is still gentle. I pray you will never learn to kill easily, even People like those two who long ago allowed their spirits to be twisted. If it's any comfort to you, you could not have helped them and they would have gone on killing as long as they lived. Now they have returned to life's most basic potential, pure energy. Remember the words of the ancient one in the cave. This is a time when life shrugs, and those who choose not to balance light and dark will not survive, at least not here. Now, let's rest well today. Tomorrow we return to the dancing cave for Fluffy's naming ceremony." Fluffy sighed and wondered if her new name would be Death. Right now the ceremony was not so attractive.

The little wolf cub watched and listened in stunned silence. He had understood everything!

The companions easily found food, and spent the rest of the day exploring, napping and wrapped up in their own thoughts. As the sun went down, they found places to sleep. The wolf cub curled up next to Fluffy as they settled in for the night, aching with questions. He said with excitement and some pride that he could understand the language of the heart now. "Fluffy, what are you doing? Who are these others and why do you travel together? I'm really grateful you saved me and that you are teaching me, but I don't understand why your life is so different than the one I remember from my den at home, and what it all means."

"I'm not sure what it means either little one. Teacher told us a lot the other day, but I don't really understand. When I was about your age, I was driven from my den by a great fire and never saw my pack again. Sheepdogs raised me and were very kind, but I didn't really belong there. Then one night Traveler showed up and we've been flying from one adventure to another ever since. One thing I'm pretty sure of though; however you got here, you are here and that means you are part of it all. Pretty soon they will be talking to you about discovering your purpose and your true name. Meanwhile, we can't just keep calling you 'little one'. What name did your pack give you?" "They didn't," answered the cub, feeling ashamed. "Let's fix that right now," insisted Fluffy. "I'd like to call you Star, is that ok with you?" "That's a great name," yipped the happy cub. "Hey everyone, my name is Star. You can all call me Star. Fluffy said so!" He bounded from one to the other, introducing himself proudly.

Late at night only Teacher and Fluffy remained awake. "Teacher, I had a strange thing happen when I was looking for Star's way home. There is a young, female people who has been in my dreams many times. One night we spoke, and since then I can't stop thinking about her." She told the story of finding the girl People near a lake, how they had talked, and mostly how strongly Fluffy felt connected to her. She was so sad at first, but happy once they met. Even though she left so abruptly, Fluffy could still feel her heart. "I saw her in the ceremony," continued Fluffly. "She was part of the story in Orb Weavers web in the cave. Then last night I saw her, not in a dream, but in Dream Time. Something had hurt her spirit terribly, and she disappeared. I can't find her or feel her anywhere.

"Who was she Teacher? Is she part of my purpose?" Teacher smiled at the news. "Yes, she is the one I told you about in the cave. Look for her. Extend your essence and try to touch her. She will need your encouragement for she walks a very lonely path on her way here. She has closed her heart because of the pain she felt, but if you keep calling, one day she will hear."

Growing Up

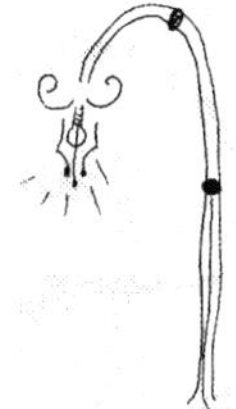

If you don't know where you're going, you can't get there. And you can't get anywhere until you know who you are.

Seneca

Beauty continued to go to church and kept her grades high. As long as she did that, her parents left her alone and she could do pretty much anything she wanted in her free time. She rode her bike alone for hours at a time. Sometimes she would get lost and get sent to bed early for not coming home on time. So, what. She had a flashlight and would read under the covers.

Once she was riding her bike on a lonely road along a river, and passed two older boys walking. They called out to her. "Hey, come on back. Come talk to us. What's your name? Do you live near here?" She turned her bike back and shyly answered their questions. She felt 'funny' around boys these days, but there was this strange attraction too. Then one of them yanked her away from her bike and started kissing her. She was in shock for a minute, then pulled away, frightened. He grabbed harder and his friend laughed. "Thinks she's too good, does she? We know you want it sweetie."

She fought free, angry now and kicking. In the struggle she fell down a bank by the river and the boys laughed and threw her bike down after her. She noticed a tiny, golden flower inches from her face. She picked it and stuck it in a braid, then, trembling with fear and anger, hauled herself to her feet and dragged her bike up the bank. It took a long time to get home that day, and she was dirty and scraped and bruised, inside as much as outside.

That summer Tatha Rose died. She went to the funeral with her family, remembering how this great aunt had fussed over her and loved her. She stood at the graveside, rigid and icy. She was the only one who didn't cry.

The year Beauty started high school, the family moved again, leaving her one good friend behind. They had moved to a new town about every four years and the isolation in which she lived grew each time. Once again, she was alone on the school grounds, the only one who didn't belong to any of the cliques, but this time boys started to notice her. Not the popular ones, they only paid attention to the clique girls. She didn't mind much. At least she wasn't always alone. She even went to the Senior Prom her freshman year. She was probably the only girl who had said yes to the young man who had crooked teeth and wore thick glasses.

High school passed in a blur. She fell for an older boy from the public school, then he graduated and joined the military. At the end of her junior year, he came back and they manipulated her parents into letting her marry him, and Beauty, barely seventeen, launched into her new life, finally free to do as she pleased.

They had fun at first. Beauty spent her days keeping house, learning to cook and reading, reading, reading. They played Hearts and Bridge with other military couples, staying up all night drinking kool aid and coffee.

None of them could afford sodas or beer, but they didn't think of themselves as poor. During five years together, two great children were born, they moved a lot, and the marriage got more and more difficult as it became clear Beauty was expected to obey her husband and never question his wishes or his behavior.

She didn't respond well, and the inevitable divorce found her back at home, with her parents and two babies. She finished high school and started college, but the relationship with her parents was terribly strained, and after a few months Beauty packed up the children and move to a small mountain town. She got a job as a waitress in a truck stop, rented a tiny house, and began two years of struggling to survive day by day.

She met some odd people in that town. They were very nice to her, but they talked about things like space beings watching over the earth, and using your mind to heal your body. It was comfortable to be with them because she was just as strange in her own way, although she never told anyone her story. One of the men was looked on as a teacher by the group, and he often held evening lessons to train people to use their minds in non-ordinary ways. They played with ESP and hyper-sentience and she tried to use it to touch other people; her childhood friends long blocked out of her mind. Beauty learned to meditate, but she was never quite sure if she was entering another dimension as she had been taught, or just falling asleep. She never did get enough sleep.

One weekend she was invited to a peyote ceremony being held at a Hogan in northern Arizona by some members of the Native American church. She had never tried drugs, mostly because there was no money and she had to take care of the kids. This was a family ceremony and everyone could bring their kids, so she jumped at it.

She was shown the right way to enter the Hogan and told this was a sacred ceremony. The purpose of the peyote was to clear the mind to come closer to the Great Spirit and seek guidance. Everyone sat around the fire, on blankets on the ground, eating the bitter peyote or drinking it as a tea. The wimps swallowed ground mushroom stuffed into gelatin capsules. The ceremony went on all night, with drumming, smudging and praying in a language she couldn't understand. Nothing happened for her except her backside hurt from sitting so long on the hard ground.

At sunrise when breakfast was being served, she asked the leader why she had not felt anything. His answer left her very sad. "Young woman, the peyote cannot touch you because your heart is closed." She knew it was true because she remembered when she made the choice. The icy coldness, which had become familiar and unnoticed through the years, returned with a sharp sting. It no longer felt so good, or at all safe. Again, an overwhelming sense of aloneness swept through her.

She left the mountain town for a city and found a job and day care for her children. Some days she could barely put one foot in front of the other. It was a dreary, grinding job, but it paid enough for them to get by. One day she was asked to work longer than usual. She needed the money, so once she made sure the sitter could keep the kids she agreed. She found herself walking home alone that night. She walked hurriedly as the evening grew darker. The fog that had softened the outlines of the city all day seemed to come alive, roiling and twisting under the street lights. She felt nervous, glancing over her shoulder often, as if to catch something moving in the deepening gloom.

There was the sound of a soft foot-pad, and suddenly a huge, black dog stood under the street light on the corner before her. It lurched and grabbed her hand in its powerful jaws, and began pulling her toward the street. The pain in her hand was fierce but she knew better than to waste any energy screaming. She fought back, kicking at the dog's legs and belly, bending over and grabbing an ear with her teeth, ripping part of it away. The vice-like grip tightened and the dog shook its head hard, attempting to throw her off balance. With her free hand she stabbed and gouged the dog's eyes, and it yowled and let go.

She stood there trembling, holding her mangled hand, as the dog slunk across the street to the opposite corner. A large woman met him under the street light and waved at him angrily to go back and get her. The shape of the dog stretched and changed, and morphed into the dark figure of a man; he stood up. His eyes were streaming blood and tears. He was weeping aloud. The woman took his arm and led him away into the fog.

She ran the few blocks home, slammed and locked the door, and dropped to a crouch on the floor, gasping in panic. How had they found her? She wasn't using the special language, in fact she could hardly remember it. She wasn't weaving things with silvery strands. She wasn't doing anything! How had they found her? Why were they coming after her? She made sure every door and window was bolted, even though it wouldn't make any difference if 'they' really wanted to come in. She thought about picking up the kids in the morning, and making a fast get-away, moving across country with bare minimum possessions. A glance at her checkbook made it clear she couldn't afford to run anywhere. Not knowing what else to do, she climbed into bed with all the lights on, pulled the covers over her head and held her sore hand close to her chest, rubbing it softly and willing it whole and well.

~~~~~~~~~~~~~~~~
~~~~~~~~~~~~~~~~

Great grandmother woke suddenly, the dream of the dog and the pain in her hand as real as the bed she was sitting on. The young woman in the dream was herself in a way, but she had never had reason to fear being hunted by anyone. It was too puzzling to contemplate, so she filed it away as "interesting". She found a robe, brushed her teeth and made some tea, then came back to sit in the chair in front of the big window in her room. From this side of the house, you could imagine there was no one else on the planet. The beautiful, rolling, green hills before her were dotted with trees and laced with a bubbling river. But there were people out there beyond her view so she began her work.

She prayed for the earth and all its children every day; not with words, but by sending out wave after wave of love. If someone walked in while she was praying, it looked like streams of golden light pouring out of her and bathing the world as far as one could see. When questioned about the shining light, great grandmother would say, "Well, I don't know about that. I'm just sending lots of love."

But this morning, thoughts of the young woman who was and wasn't her were haunting her. Was there someone to love her? Did she have family and friends? An ache in her heart told her of the great loneliness and fear clutching Beauty's essence. She decided this morning her love would fold and wrap around the young woman, and stay there until she found peace and comfort. She brought an image of her, standing in the fog and clutching her wounded hand, into the center of her mind/heart/spirit, and poured the wealth of her love. She sent the love streaming into everywhere and everywhen the young woman would live. The golden waves pulsed out of her and spiraled across time and space, carrying a magical and haunting melody.

~~~~~~~~~~~~~~~~

The years went on, and Beauty moved from one relationship to another, in an effort to erase the loneliness. Each one was worse than the last. Finally at 38, children grown and gone, she found herself alone in another new mountain town, starting life all over again. Since the night of peyote she had been searching for something to fill the emptiness, and was willing to listen to almost anything as long as the word "God" wasn't mentioned. Again she met some nice but strange people. Everyone was looking for an answer or some meaning in a world that just didn't fit them. Some called themselves energy healers, some psychics or card readers. One did Kirlian photography.

Beauty tried it all, and one night during some "energy work" a memory popped in. She was in that cold room with bright lights and white tile walls, helpless and kicking in the new infant body. The large, black shape was pressing the center of her forehead with a thumb and roaring "NO!" The memory left her shaken, her armor cracked. That night, dreaming she was asleep on a narrow bed, a beautiful, sleek wolf approached and laid its head on her hand. The warm, soft eyes looked at her, and she felt so safe and nurtured she fell into a deep, dreamless sleep for the first time in several years. She slept 14 hours that night, and every night for three weeks, waking each morning with a startled jolt, and dragging through each day exhausted. Finally one morning she woke rested and in a wonderful mood. Something was stirring in her heart; a faint tendril of opening to feelings she had blocked away for years. She knew somehow that life was different now and she would be OK.
~~~~~~~~~~~~~~~~

Awakening

It's really a wonder that I haven't dropped all my ideals, because they seem so absurd and impossible to carry out. Yet I keep them, because in spite of everything I still believe that people are really good at heart.

Anne Frank

She scrambled up the rocky hillside carrying a beach towel, a thermos of iced tea and a book. It was a clear, warm day with a lovely breeze. The dry air of the high desert was fresh from a rare shower, and small puddles of water collected in the hollows of rocks. The patch of grass at the top of the hill was still spring green, softly welcoming her as she spread her towel, dropped her book and thermos and peeled off the light cotton sundress. Her skin was nut brown from glorious days like this, and her dark hair took on a reddish sheen.

She stretched out on the towel. The book was ignored as she slipped into a reverie, her mind playing with the possibilities she had been reading about earlier. "Is it possible to move energy and change events just by thinking about it? Could I learn to communicate just with my thoughts, or learn to heal someone? What was that swirl of lights that showed up around me in a photograph last month? Are space beings what Catholics call angels and saints? What is so special about crystals? Is there such a thing as sacred places on the earth?" She chuckled at that thought. She was laying in a sacred place. At least, it seemed so.

She slipped further into peacefulness, eyes open but unfocused. The air filled with countless tiny sparkling lights. Blinking to clear her vision, she realized it wasn't just dust motes dancing in the sun, but a growing cloud of glowing bits of .....what? Her perception shifted slightly and she realized the lights weren't just in the air. They were in and through everything. Rocks, water, towel, herself, everything. She suddenly touched a well of happiness deep inside her that was sweeter than anything she had ever experienced. Joy was breathing her. She held perfectly still, afraid it would slip away.

She felt like she was expanding, merging her essence with all that surrounded her. She felt rock and knew grass and flew moth. A dragon fly landed on her toe, and she felt a surge like an electric shock, bursting out laughing in delight. She felt new and soft, yet strong as the rocks surrounding her. A sweet scent filled her nose, and a lavender rose appeared right in front of her. She suddenly remembered everything she had closed off and forgotten since she was twelve. Memories of spiders and silver strands, the shining one and her three friends, and a beautiful wolf came flooding in as though they happened this morning. Thinking of the long conversations with Spider brought tears to her eyes, and oh, how she longed to ride a rainbow and sprinkle stardust.

Thinking of mommy still held an aching loneliness, and the large black shape that pursued her brought a shiver of fear. Remembering the priest who had told her God didn't want girls, that she was trafficking with the devil and committing a sin of pride, started the old anger roiling up. She shouted "NO" and blew the anger out of her body with three great breaths when she realized the anger was stealing her joy. "NO! Nothing, no one will ever steal my joy again. This is my heart, my mind, my body. I choose what I allow in. She relaxed and the joy came streaming back in, this time strong and certain. It belonged to her now. She had claimed it and would explore its depths.

She slipped easily back into her reverie, expanding her essence. It was an adventure of discovery. Every new life form she touched had its own unique pattern. Bushes and lichen and rocks all had their own breath, slower but no less powerful than insects or animals or her own breath. Suddenly Beauty knew the full meaning of "children of the earth" and she was filled with love.

Once again, life was different. She was different.

Beauty went to visit her parents. It was almost a perverse testing of whether she would allow anyone to steal her joy. They exchanged the latest news over dinner, then Mom began her usual litany of "How could you, why didn't you, you should." With a sigh of resignation, Beauty got up to clear the dishes, the strident words following her. Then a miracle happened. Dad reached over, patted Mom's hand. "Honey, she's not like us. She is different. You've got to let her go. She has to follow her own heart." With a jolt of returning joy, Beauty realized her father had truly seen her and even approved of her. The ache she carried around her family was eased. Compassion was born in her heart for her mother, and grateful love for her father.

The change in Beauty brought a profound change in the people in her life. Her blossoming compassion and kindness drew men and women who were struggling and wanting life to get better. She found part time work assisting in a seminar that was designed to help people awaken to their own spirits. She practiced expanding her essence so she could feel the needs in others. She found she was gifted in leading others in visualization exercises, and used the metaphors of nature for comfort and healing. She remembered how to feel and see music as well as hear it, and began to understand its profound effect on everyone's heart and spirit.

At the end of a seminar when everyone else had gone home, Margie came to her, devastated and despairing over the ending of her thirty year marriage. She had devoted her whole life as wife and mother. Even her friends were in her life because of her husband's business or her children's activities. The children were grown and gone, and now her husband had left her. She was bereft of family, stripped of pride, and terrified of a future that appeared blank and hopeless.

"Margie," Beauty invited, "close your eyes and follow my voice. Take all the time you need to feel and hear and smell what I say. Ready? You are a stalk of wheat in a field. It is a cloudy autumn day. Your stalk is your marriage and the leaves on the side your children. Your energy, your essence is flowing through the stalk and the leaves, nurturing them and helping them grow. But you grow beyond them, bursting into blossom, then releasing the blossom and becoming seed.

A harvester comes along and cuts away the stalk and the leaves, and you, the seed, are dropped to the ground. You don't even make it to the threshing floor or the flour mill. You are just dropped in the dirt. It begins to rain. Dirt washes over you, and you are buried alone in the cold, wet earth. It gets colder and the ground freezes. Hell has frozen over for you. You wait, and listen in the cold, wet darkness. Then it warms again. The sun penetrates the earth and your hard, red shell cracks open. Your roots anchored firmly in the rich soil of your past, you launch a new shoot toward the sun. You are born again, into a new, glorious life."

She put on a recording of Bette Midler's 'The Rose', pulled Margie to her feet and the two of them danced around the room, singing the verses with tears streaming and faces smiling. Margie was already getting ideas about the future she could create for herself. Beauty reached an even deeper understanding that there was no separation between her own essence and that of any part of life. It all vibrated around her, waiting only her open heart to touch her.

It was a year before she saw Margie again, this time glowing with energy and happiness. She had allowed the hard shell of her heart to crack open and was creating the life of her dreams.

~~~~~~~~~~~~~~~~

Coming home one night, Beauty noticed a grey cat huddled on her front porch. She stepped around it into the house, expecting it to run home. It began to mewl weakly at the closed door and she could feel the creature tugging at her heart. She opened the door. The cat was filthy, it's long fur matted and tangled, and so thin its bones were poking out. She couldn't turn him away. He had no claws so he couldn't hunt for food or defend himself. It took days to cut away the mats and clean the fur, which turned out to be pure white. His eyes were bright green and crossed with a fine, golden web. No matter how much he ate, he stayed bony. A vet said he was basically healthy, but , as improbable as it sounds, the webbing over his eyes made it likely he was around twenty five years old, so he probably would not gain weight.

Beauty named him Sam, but somehow couldn't help calling him Bones. They became fast friends. He stayed
~~~~~~~~~~~~~~~~

skinny but his coat grew back shiny and silky. Bones slept tucked into her shoulder, and would wake her by patting her chin or running one of his long whiskers up her nose. She would squeal at the intense tickle, and Bones would head for the food dish.

Sometimes he would stare at her, head cocked, as though waiting for her to do or say something, and she would try. "What do you want Bones? More water? Do you want to cuddle?" He would strain toward her, as though he could encourage her to speak more clearly or hear what he was saying. Her throat would sometimes ache with the effort and she often had the odd feeling she was hanging right at the edge of something.

One night Beauty picked up Bones and held him in her lap as she curled into a lawn chair under the stars. "Bones, I want to tell you a story. I hope you can understand at least the feeling if not the words. When I was a little girl, I had a Spider friend. We could speak and understand each other perfectly well. Spider taught me we are all children of the earth, and it makes sense that we could understand each other. She also taught me how important it is to be respectful and take care not to harm each other. She told me everyone has a purpose, and when I discovered my true purpose, I would have a naming ceremony. My new name would tell everyone what my purpose it. She promised she would be there for the ceremony, but that was many years ago, and spiders don't live that long. Sometimes I feel I have failed her by not discovering my purpose soon enough. Now I can't even remember how to speak that special language. I'm so sorry. I wish you and I could share our thoughts that way."

She told Bones about how she had closed her heart and shut out everyone, and how much she regretted all she had lost by doing that. "But you are here and you are helping me to love more and more. I'm so glad you are my friend." The two sat content under the stars until sleep began to take over, then went to bed, Bones curled happily into Beauty's shoulder. As she drifted off to sleep, she dreamed again of a great cave. She saw everything. The firelight, the dancers, the old man. There were drums and a flute playing as the dancers leaped and turned. A flash of silver caught her eye and she glanced up to find a great Spider weaving beautiful strands. Everything in her strained toward the spider, but it didn't respond. Then the dancers turned, and there was wolf. They moved closer together and Beauty reached out to touch the quarter-moon burn scar on the wolf's hip. A sense of strength and peace and safety poured into her.

She woke with a start in the deep of night, realizing Bones wasn't there. Gripped with a fearful premonition, she searched the house, then the neighborhood, calling his name far into the night. Finally surrendering to his loss, she pealed his name one last time, from the very depths of her soul. BONES!!!! Where are you? BONES!!!! The earth rocked at the power of her call, but she didn't notice. The dream of the wolf was forgotten, although the outline of a quarter moon marked her palm. Hot tears and the stabbing pain in her heart were all she knew that night. Bones was gone as suddenly as he had come.

Sasha

There is more to us than we know. If we can be made to see it, perhaps for the rest of our lives we will be unwilling to settle for less.

Kurt Hahn

The next morning as they prepared to travel to the cave, their resting place was suddenly filled with crows; cawing, flapping, feeding and flying back and forth. Teacher held out an arm which was soon occupied by one of the crows. The two stared intently at each other for a minute, then the crow flew off. Teacher bowed solemnly, reached deep in a pocket and pulled out a handful of dried corn which he cast on the ground. The group mounted to the sky, watching the crows feeding happily on the corn. Traveler with his three riders, and Messenger flew through unseasonable thunderheads. "Fly swiftly," Teacher called to Messenger and Traveler. "I'm holding the picture of our cave alive in my mind. Get us there as fast as you can." Lightning flashed around them and they were jolted by the percussion of loud claps following each flash. The light was eerie and yellowish. It felt other-worldly, as though they had slipped into some strange reality. Fluffy noticed that Teacher and Messenger were worried but didn't dare ask why. Traveler just kept setting the pace, keeping them moving swiftly toward the hills with the dancing cave. Star kept his head down, whimpering a bit.

They reached the cave just as great balls of hail came crashing out of the sky, spitting flecks of water and shards of ice as they broke open on the rocks. Ducking inside, the sound of the hail was thunderous and the wind screeched like an enraged banshee. Thunder claps reverberated off the walls of the cave and twisting lightning flickered so they all looked like they were in a macabre dance. The air was acrid and sulfurous. Fluffy's throat closed with a reflexive memory of the great fire.

They sat for a few minutes to catch their breaths, especially the goose and the eagle. "What happened?" cried Messenger. "I've never seen such a vile storm. There was something very wrong about it. Something unnatural." Teacher nodded. "It was unnatural. The crows came to warn us that it was brewing and we had to travel fast to escape it. We wouldn't have made it without their warning. That hail was big enough to kill a bull, and it had other dangerous components. Did you notice the smell?" They looked around at each other with their eyes wide, nodding. "There was a chemical component in that hail," Teacher continued. "I don't know what it is, but anything that smells that bad is telling you it's dangerous."

"But why?" asked Fluffy. "Did someone make that happen? Who has that kind of power? Was it just in our path or was it actually after us? Why would anyone do something like that? Are we still in danger? Will it happen again? What if we don't get a warning next time?" This time her companions didn't mock her, but waited for her flurry of questions to wind down. Teacher continued his explanation. "The crows told me there are those who know we came here for Fluffy's naming ceremony, and they don't want it to happen, so they wanted to kill us or at least scare us off. They are afraid of Fluffy's power becoming strong enough to harm them if she discovers her true name and purpose. They will be watching closely for her, trying to get her again. So far they don't seem to give the rest of us much importance. We have to keep it that way. We don't want to be discovered or our usefulness will be lost, and we need to help keep Fluffy hidden as much as possible. This cave is shielded by the ancient ones, so no one out there can feel our presence unless we invite them."

"Will I have a stronger power after my naming?" asked Fluffy. "More than one," was the response. "And the more you use them, the stronger they will get." Fluffy looked dejected. "Yesterday I used my power to kill a man. I still feel soiled." Teacher's response was firm and loud. "You used your power yesterday to save a man's life; mine. Let me show you a picture!" A horrific sight filled Fluffy's eyes. Teacher was laying on the ground, ribbons of flesh cut from his arms and chest. Two fingers were bleeding stumps, and his throat was slashed. He was quite dead. Fluffy retched, and a searing pain stabbed her heart as the vision faded. "How do you know that would have happened?" she cried.

Teacher stood, his arms outstretched as though pleading. "Time is not linear and reality is not fixed. It is possible to see into other dimensions. Remember that. One day it will help you when you have to make some hard decisions. You can look at probable outcomes by extending your energy much as you find your way in your earthly travels. It crossed my mind to stop you and Messenger from killing those two men, but I looked at probable futures and saw they would cause many brutal deaths if they recovered. My friend, I will always be grateful to you for defending me. You must let go of the idea you did anything wrong."

The storm passed and the early afternoon sun came out. The rocks were scarred and chipped where the hail had hit and some low bushes were splintered, but everything else looked normal. The acrid smell dissipated quickly in the dry, desert breeze. The companions brought more wood to the cave from the river at the foot of the hill. Teacher insisted on a good supply. Tonight's ceremony might be long. They found food and did their best to calm their ragged nerves and nap, in preparation for a long night of ceremony.

As the sun finally set, Teacher built a small fire in the center of the cave. He performed a gratitude ritual, sprinkling the remaining ash he had gathered from the last fire over this new one. "Thank you, kind fire, for giving me your ash, which helped save my life from the two killers. I am grateful for your wood which sacrifices itself, for your heat which warms us, for your light to see by, and for your ash which sweetens life in so many ways. I promise to use the gift of fire always for the good of all the children of the earth." Teacher bowed solemnly, took out his pipe and lit it with a brand from the fire, then joined the smoke of his pipe with the smoke of the fire. The two clouds of smoke curled together, upward through the vent in the cave roof, and spread out toward the stars, carrying the prayer of gratitude through space and time.

The flames lit the cave wall with its paintings of sun and corn and humans and creatures. "Let us begin our ceremony," said Teacher. He brought out his drum and Traveler began the dance. The paintings stirred and dancers left the walls and circled the fire. The rhythm of the drum increased, the flute wove in a happy tune and the dance became one of joyful celebration, the movements telling stories of travels and courage and friendship and courtship.

They danced a great, ancient elk hunt, feeling the happiness that came with the knowledge they would have enough for the winter. They danced to honor and thank the elk spirits, promising to pray for their descendants. As they finished dancing and sat in a circle around the fire, Traveler walked around it, indicating he would tell the next story. He spoke in the language of the children of the earth, and everyone could understand, even young Star. "My friend, this wolf and I were on a journey and we found an infant People, lost and alone. It was filthy and bad smelling and very frightened. Fluffy insisted we help it get home, even though I explained the People were very dangerous, particularly to wolves found near their young. She refused to leave him, because he would die out there alone. So she followed the child's scent and I nipped at it from behind to keep it moving. We found his home, and the grown People had a gun and came after her to kill her. He chased us for a long time." Traveler then danced the story, causing laughter when he mimicked pecking at the baby's soggy drawers, and more laughter when he danced as Fluffy, making awful faces while sniffing to find the way. "My wolf friend risked her life to protect the life of a People," finished Traveler. An ancient man with long, white hair stood and threw something on the fire. It flashed and sent sparks to the cave roof, where the great Orb Weaver caught a spark and created a new strand in the story of the web of life.

Then it was Teacher's turn. He told the story of the cruel men taunting him and how Fluffy had attacked at exactly the right moment to protect his life. "She used her essence to feel what was happening, and knew when to move and how to bring down the man with the knife." Teacher then danced the story, on all fours at first, slinking out of the woods and circling till the time was right. Then he danced her great leap, bringing the man down with one snap of her powerful jaws. "My wolf friend risked her life to protect my life," said Teacher.

Again the ancient man threw something on the fire, and again sparks rose to Orb Weaver. Another strand was woven in the web of life. Then he came toward Fluffy with a stone bowl full of burning sweet grass and a feather fan. Fluffy willed herself to be calm at the scent of burning grass and stood still as she was bathed in smoke from nose to tail tip. The old man spoke for the first time. "Young wolf, do you now understand your purpose? Your mother taught you the language of the heart so you could speak to all beings. You were called away from her den to take your place among those who work to bring the light back into balance. You learned skills from your friends. You used your heart and your skills to protect the lives of two People. This is your purpose. I name you Sasha, Protector of Humans."

Fluffy was startled. The only kind human she had met was Teacher, unless you count the young girl coming to her in dreams and visions. "All people?" she asked with a quavering voice. The ancient one shook his head. "Only those who are helping to bring the light and dark back into balance. Right now they are few and not strong. The child you returned to his home is one of them. There is a female People you will defend across time and space. One day she will be your closest companion and the two of you will fulfill a great mission together, but until she discovers her name and her true purpose, she will need your help. Now, you must begin to use your true name. It will make you stronger."

He called to the watching circle. "Let us dance Sasha!" The flute and drum began again; the figures around the fire sprang to life and danced in celebration around Sasha. Gourd rattles were shaken back and forth across her body. Teacher rubbed warm ashes into the old scar on her rump.

She felt it tighten and change. She joined the dancers, leaping around the circle as they sang her name aloud. "Sasha, Sasha." The rightness of it settled into her heart, and with her whole being, she uttered a mighty "YES!"

As the dancing ended, Sasha respectfully approached the ancient one in the red blanket. "The female People I am to protect, is there some way I can help her now, before we become companions?" asked Sasha. "Call to her. Call her spirit here for a blessing," was the reply. "The scar on your hip is a powerful talisman you will share." A rough, white quarter moon shape had risen on her rump. Sasha extended her awareness, making space for an image in his mind. A grown woman with dark hair and eyes, nut brown skin and a solemn face materialized out of the smoke. She could feel Beauty's kind heart, and also feel her deep loneliness. Their eyes met, then the woman touched her scar, and Sasha knew in a flash the depth of their connection. Teacher used the feather and stone bowl to bathe her in sacred smoke, and the ancient one rattled the gourd all around her. She put her hands to her mouth for a moment, then with a sad smile, turned and was gone.

The music came to an end. The dancers withdrew until only their painted figures on the walls remained. "Lets sleep if we can," said Teacher. "Tomorrow we plan more training, and that means travel." Not yet certain of the safety outside the cave, they curled up on the dirt floor as comfortably as possible, and slept easily and dreamlessly.

In the morning Teacher's jaw was tight with determination, and he spoke commandingly. "I have spent the night in Dream Time, and the holy one traveled with me. Changes are coming much faster than we expected, so we must prepare without delay. Messenger, go find the Searchers and send them to me. We have to find that female human and help her. The dark ones know who she is and how to find her. She has closed her heart and that will protect her for a while, but they will track her down eventually. We must find her first. Then go back to your nest. Another call is coming for you soon."

"Sasha and Traveler," continued Teacher, "you have a long and dangerous mission. You must learn your way to and from anywhere on this planet. The time is coming when you will have to blink in and out of places in a heartbeat and you must have sensed every one of them first in order to do that safely. Use the 'finding' instinct of both goose and wolf, and teach each other all you learn. You will have to run and fly and 'turn' in time and space. Learn to camouflage your actions and if you are spotted, be careful to hide your partnership and your abilities, even from those who appear friendly or neutral. Travel cautiously and stay hidden. The dark ones don't know what you can do yet and we need to keep it that way. No heroics please, just 'find' all the times and places of the earth. Well, at least as many as possible."

"What about you, Teacher?" asked Traveler. "Shall I fly you to your home first?" "My home is my campfire and my pipe. I will stay here for now," was Teacher's reply. The four looked at each other solemnly, then bowed in respect. "Remember, you can search and 'find' me wherever I am now that you know my essence." Messenger left first, his great wings beating the air till the dust on the ground swirled. Traveler and Sasha decided they would fly together until they reached unfamiliar territory, then come up with a plan. With a final salute to Teacher, Sasha got on Travelers back and they soared skyward. Teacher watched till they slipped out of sight, then returned to the cave.

Mapping

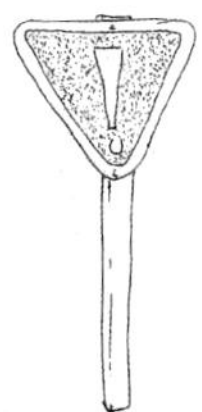

We don't accomplish anything in this world alone... and whatever happens is the result of the whole tapestry of one's life and all the weavings of individual threads from one to another that creates something.

Sandra Day O'Connor

The friends flew in a back and forth pattern, sometimes turning in time and space, sometimes walking together. They were very cautious around farms and small towns and along People roads. One early morning they turned a corner in a village and bumped into a pair of People weaving precariously as they walked. They watched in fascination as they were examined by the wobbly twosome, wondering what made them so unsteady. Suddenly one of the drunks seemed to snap awake and screamed, "WOLF." Traveler and Sasha quickly 'turned' to another space, leaving the men to argue about what they had or had not seen.

As they traveled, both of them concentrated on extending their senses, absorbing all they found. When they stopped for rest or food they would share everything they had found. They soon realized this was taking far too long.

They weren't covering nearly enough territory, so they decided to separate during the day and find each other by feel at night. They mapped a lot more of the land that way.

One night as Sasha extended her senses to find Traveler, she felt an unpleasant tingle pass over her. Looking around, it seemed there was a dark shape moving toward her. She suddenly remembered Teacher's warnings about staying hidden and quickly snapped all her energy back into her body, making it small and still as possible. She waited motionless until the shape passed over her and kept moving. She waited another hour, then another before trying again to find Traveler. In an instant Traveler's warning, "HIDE" flashed in her, and she dove for a low bush; hunkering down, hardly breathing.

The dark shape passed over her twice more and now she could faintly feel its probe as it searched for her. She slowed her essence to match that of rock, and didn't move again for two days. When she cautiously emerged she could not sense anything unusual. She considered 'seeking' Traveler just as his message popped into her awareness. The touch was brief as a blink, but it was enough. She knew exactly where to go to find him. She hoped no one or nothing else caught the same message.

Sasha kept near a tree line as she sought Traveler. She moved carefully, but kept her senses somewhat extended, gathering information. She began to notice something different, perhaps triggered by the jolt of seeing the dark shape. She had always been able to sense that each place had its own feel, but now she was more acutely aware of the quality of the feeling.

Most places were quite ordinary with no particular quality, but some places seemed to carry a history of events. One felt heavy and cold with sorrow. Some actually made her skin crawl, as though terrible deeds had been committed there and the very ground was saturated with them. One was bursting with life and excitement. "Taste me! Try me!" she heard it call. Another drew her into a sense of the sacred; very similar to what she had felt in the great cave. Teacher's words, "be careful to hide," echoed in her memory. Was there a way she could pass without leaving an imprint of her presence on the land?

Sasha moved into the Silence as she walked, examining imprints left by others. She sent out a wisp of thought in an attempt to erase one, but it didn't work. Another wisp of thought moved two imprints together, and both changed. Here was her solution! If she moved carefully *through* other imprints, it would mask her passing. She practiced a bit, then picked up her pace in search of Traveler, eager to test her idea. The two rejoined that night, both with a huge amount of information to share.

The next morning they flew to a quiet glade with a dark, heavy quality to its feel. Sasha crossed it once and Traveler had no difficulty finding her. Then she went to another spot in the glade and carefully moved *through* the imprints she found. It worked. Traveler lost her, and she had to retrace her steps and find him. But there was a major problem. Moving *through* the imprints left a heavy energy on Sasha's spirit. It took her hours to rid herself of it and feel whole again. The friends decided this method of travel would only be used in the most dire circumstances. They continued their searching, mood subdued by the thought of the dark shape that had spotted Sasha. The same darkness knew about the dark haired girl. It was worrisome.

After some time Traveler and Sasha settled at the edge of a farm field, near a large rock surrounded by bushes. It would make good cover. Irregular shapes poked at the sky near the horizon. "What is that?" asked Sasha. "They are called buildings. We are approaching a place where a great many of the People live. We will have to be very careful not to be seen. They are used to seeing geese, but you would cause a panic, and that means guns. People will be our greatest danger here. We'll go at night and stay in the shadows." They rested as the sun set and lights came on in the city. Sasha thought about Beauty. He searched for her and called her every day, but always there was no reply. Again tonight the call went out and found nothing. When some of the lights began to turn off again, they headed for the city.

They used their senses cautiously, walking close to buildings. They had agreed to fly only if necessary, and to be prepared to 'turn' at any moment. A swirling fog helped mask their passing; still they avoided being caught in any light. Crossing the city in wide paths, they were easily able to map the energy patterns. Both of them had gotten so good at 'finding' there was no need to make a great effort to remember. Once an area was sensed, it became a permanent memory. Sasha had never been in a city before. She decided to try calling Beauty, softly and cautiously. She sent out her awareness and searched for her, and this time felt a ripple of something. She couldn't identify what she felt, but her awareness was heightened.

Sasha and Traveler turned a corner and there she was, walking along and looking over her shoulder. As she stepped into the light of a street lamp, a large, black dog attacked, snarling as it grabbed her hand. Traveler's whispered "stop!" was so strong that Sasha instantly obeyed, but argued, "she's in danger. We have to help." "Wait," was the reply. "We might make it worse if we reveal ourselves."

They watched the struggle from the shadows. It seemed to go on forever, but it was barely a minute. The dog ran away, whimpering and met a woman dressed in black on the opposite corner. It stood up and turned into the shape of a man, and the two moved away into the darkness. Traveler held Sasha back by sheer force of will. "Wait. She looks like she's ok. Let's follow her but stay hidden."

Beauty clutched her wounded hand to her chest and began to run. They followed her until she ran into a building and slammed the door. Sasha sent her awareness after Beauty and was shocked at her fear and anguish, and was even more shocked that she couldn't feel anything else. She couldn't feel the young woman's heart! Only a sensation of cold, slick steel. Traveler felt the same thing, and they had no idea what to do. There was no way to communicate if you couldn't feel someone's heart. They watched, hoping she would come out again, but soon all the lights inside went out and all was silent. They were wondering what to do when a soft, golden light streamed into the building. It was beautiful and nurturing and warm. "Let's go," said Traveler. "She'll be OK now."

They slipped out of the city as dawn was breaking, returning to their hiding place in the farm field. Sasha circled the rock, trying to think and work off her agitation. Had her searching led the man and woman of the darkness to Beauty? Who was the woman and how did the dog become a man? She longed to ask Teacher, but they still had too far to go to turn back now. She became convinced she had alerted the dark ones to Beauty's location, and guilt washed over her. In an attempt to cheer Sasha, Traveler talked about how well Beauty fought; how wise she was to go for the dog's weakest spot, its eyes. "And don't forget the light. You saw that golden light. I don't know what it is, but it's watching over her. I just know she's going to be fine." Sasha kept seeing the dog lunge and Traveler couldn't console her.

"I want to go back at night and get her. At least if we stay close we can protect her," said Sasha. "It won't work.

We can't talk to her because her heart is closed and we can't fix that. She has to do it herself. She would just be afraid of us and that wouldn't help anything. Then if we got spotted we would be in trouble, and what about the mission Teacher gave us? We have a long way to go. We can't let everyone down. Maybe Beauty has to walk her lonely path to discover her purpose. We wouldn't want to wreck that for her." Sasha knew Traveler was right. They better get some rest so they could continue 'finding' for Teacher.

In the Garden

To see a world in a grain of sand, and a heaven in a wildflower... hold infinity in the palm of your hand, and eternity in an hour...

William Blake

They did go back to the city the next evening, but this time Traveler carried Sasha and flew, turning them through different times and dimensions. There was no sign of Beauty in any of them. They got some dogs barking, but no People spotted them, and the darkness didn't appear to be present. Sasha's heart was not in 'finding'. She couldn't get Beauty out of her mind. Traveler decided they both could use a rest, and searched for a place that felt right, then 'turned' them into a lush garden. A lion was waiting for them.

"Welcome, children of the earth. You can rest safely here. My home is shielded from uninvited outsiders. You are Traveler and Sasha. Well named, both of you. Some are already beginning to talk about the mapping you are doing. It will make a huge difference when the Change comes. For now, rest and ask for anything you need. Let's start with food, shall we?" The pond was rich with Traveler's favorite food and he set to it with relish. The gardens were a hunter's paradise, but Sasha was troubled.

"Great Lion, all the children of the earth in your garden have the language of the heart. I have never killed one of these for food."

"Ahh, you still believe life can end," said the lion. "Perhaps I can offer you some lessons about that. For now, please understand the food you take in this garden is here for you by conscious choice. They know they will become a part of your essence, and therefore have a part in restoring the balance of light and dark. You have a great work to do and they are eager to help. Take all you want, and do it with a blessing and gratitude. All is well." Sasha did as she was told, placing particular focus on gratitude, and the food she ate nourished her body and somehow strengthened her soul.

Sasha walked back to the pond and found Traveler and the lion. Traveler flapped his wings with importance. "Sasha, let me introduce you properly. This lion is Ariel, but you are looking at much more than a lion. It appears Ariel is not limited by time, dimension, gender or species. Ariel, please show my friend what you showed me. She's not going to believe it! She's not going to believe it!" The goose was bouncing and cackling with excitement.

The lion lifted her front paws then rose on her hind legs. A very tall woman with long robes and a mass of golden brown hair stood before them. Traveler's antics and the stunned look on Sasha's face brought a chuckle from her throat. His/her voice remained the same; warm and welcoming.

"My name is always Ariel, whatever form I'm in. Now that you know me, I will come whenever you call. Sasha, you carry a heaviness in your heart. You are worried about someone?" Sasha told about her deep connection to the human woman, losing contact with Beauty because she had closed herself off. "Do you really want to help her?"

asked Ariel. "Well, yes, of course I do," responded Sasha. "Then you must learn to manage the energy of your essence and keep it clean and helpful. If you are willing, follow me."

She led them deeper into the garden, to a huge sunflower. "Sasha, when you fly with Traveler sometimes he 'turns' you into another time or dimension. We are going to practice fast forwarding and backtracking in time until you get comfortable with it. Settle into Silence now, and feel what it's like to 'turn'."

Sasha complied, practicing the feeling until she nearly blinked out of view. "Good, very good," said Ariel, catching her just in time and holding her present. "Now, keep part of your focus on me so I can track 'when' you are. See if you can notice two different threads of energy, one crossing dimensions and another crossing times." Again Sasha focused inward, noticing for the first time the powerful forces at her disposal. There was just the faintest difference between the two, a slight twist in a thread, but it was unmistakable.

"Keep your focus on me Sasha. Follow the time thread back three days, then immediately turn back to now." Ariel concentrated intently on Sasha, and for a brief second both woman and wolf blinked out of that time, then back in. "Now we will fast forward one week, then come back here." "But how?" Sasha protested. "I know what three days ago was like and it was easy to find, but a week in the future is a mystery. I don't know what to look for."

The great mane of golden brown hair seemed electrified as Ariel extended her energy and surrounded Sasha, as though to directly transmit her own understanding. "There is only now. There is no such thing as linear time. The children of the earth made it up to play with. You can use this funny toy by simply deciding 'when' you want to be. It is all done by focusing your essence with intention. Let's try it. I'll go with you, and I want you to focus on this sunflower and notice if anything seems different."

Again Sasha and Ariel blinked out of view for just a flash, then blinked back in. Traveler was flapping his wings and squawking in delight, proud of how quickly his friend learned. Ariel was complimentary but very serious. "You did very well Sasha. Do you think you can do it on your own now?" "Oh, yes," was the surprised reply. "It is very much like sending out my essence to find a place. And I noticed the sunflower stalk had another blossom on it."

Ariel sighed. "Good. One day it may be very useful as you travel, but for now it has a more serious use. We are going to use it to teach you the consequences of your thoughts and how to manage the personal energy you extend to others. Do you still feel the heavy energy of worry about the female human?" Sasha nodded. "Then gather every bit of that worry from wherever it is, inside or outside your body, and focus it right here." She held her hands in front of the wolf, about six inches apart, as though about to catch a ball.

Slipping back into the Silent space, Sasha concentrated until she could feel something move from her to Ariel's waiting hands. "Good, now give that energy to the sunflower." Sasha complied, wondering if the female human liked flowers, and whether they were going to send her this one. "Come, fast forward a week again with me, and find the sunflower," commanded Ariel. Sasha gasped. The two blossoms on the sunflower were drooping. The leaves were turning yellow and the plant looked wilted. "It's dying!" cried Sasha. "Let's go back," was the terse reply. "Now, gather the happiest memory you have of her from inside and outside your body, and tell me when you're ready."

Sasha remembered meeting at the lake, promising to help each other discover their true names. It had felt so right. When she nodded her readiness, Ariel said, "pour that energy, the essence of that memory, into the sunflower. Fill it up." Sasha obeyed, and at Ariel's command the two of them again leaped into next week. The sunflower was thriving, its stalk strong and bearing yet another flower, and its leaves crisp and green. Sasha was so stunned Ariel yanked him back to the time where Traveler waited.

"Do you understand?" whispered Ariel. "I nearly killed the sunflower, then somehow I healed it. Was it really all from my thoughts?" asked Sasha. "Yes, and you have the same effect on anyone or anything. Your thoughts are your greatest responsibility. If you are sending thoughts of concern or fear for your friend, you are sapping her strength no matter how good your intentions. If you are going to defend her, gather thoughts of power and safety and confidence until you can feel them in your body, then send her that energy essence." Sasha thought a moment. "She carried such a sad loneliness. I wish I could send her joy." "Then pick an image that represents joy to you, hold on to it clearly until you can feel it, and send it to her on the wings of your intentions," was Ariel's advice.

Sasha noticed a brilliant dragonfly glinting in the sunshine as it flitted about the garden. It landed on the sunflower and Sasha felt the happiness of knowing the plant was whole and well. Joy was bubbling up inside her and she couldn't tell if it was coming from her or the dragonfly, but it didn't matter. Joy kept building until the intensity felt like a shock, then she sent it spinning, dragonfly and all, across times and dimensions, holding a picture of Beauty firmly in her mind. She looked at Ariel with gratitude shining out of her eyes. Traveler raised his wings, basking in the magic. "That's quite a day's work," said Ariel. Let's head for the porch. A tall, cold drink is in order." Her hand patted Sasha's rump as though to say, "well done."

As they relaxed on the porch, Sasha's curiosity was piqued. "Traveler, have you been here before? How did you know to come here?" "My parents dropped me off here when they finished raising me. They said it was for my education. This is where I learned to 'turn' in time and space, and how to carry passengers and loads much larger than myself. Ariel taught me, but it was much different. She let in a People with a cold and vicious heart so I would learn to spot his kind from a distance and avoid them. He didn't speak our language, but he had so much power he was terrifying."

Ariel broke in. "Actually, that's not totally accurate. The man's name is Gene and he doesn't have a drop of cruelty in his heart. He is a great actor though, and very powerful at managing his essence. Sorry to have tricked you that way, but you weren't taking anything seriously. You were too busy clowning to learn much, and I had to scare you to get your attention. I probably shouldn't tell you this, but the two of us would roll on the floor laughing after we sent you off to rest. If you're thinking of revenge, Traveler," she said with a knowing look, "first remember how well those lessons have served you."

If a goose could pout……. Sasha broke in. "He saved my life more than once using what you and Gene taught him. And he may be a clown, but he's the best friend anyone could ever have." Ariel nodded. "We saw his loyalty and courage at once. That's why we spent so much time and effort with him." Looking gently at Traveler, she continued, "The clowning is not a bad thing, it is one of your gifts. You are able to lift others hearts and remind them of the goodness of life when all they can see is sorrow and darkness. Please don't stop clowning, just use it with wisdom." Traveler looked appeased. "So, where is this People named Gene? Maybe I can come up with a bit of revenge without doing any harm." "He's down by the riverbank fishing. Probably napping, actually." Traveler couldn't contain a grin. "See ya later," he called, and blinked out of their space.

Traveler lit on a tree branch just above the sleeping man. He plucked out a loose feather, flew silently to the ground and shape shifted. He bent over the skinny figure and tickled his nose with the feather. Gene woke with a start, then screamed at the sight of a four hundred pound goose with a feather in his beak standing over him. Traveler blinked back to his normal size and rolled on the ground, choking with laughter. Gene fumed for a minute, then dissolved in chuckles, proud of his former student. When they caught their breaths, the two of them headed for the porch in the garden.

Ariel and Sasha were deep in conversation about Beauty and their relationship. "Soon this female People and you will travel many of the spaces that you and Traveler have mapped. The two of you will gather those that Teacher and others like him have prepared, and lead them to a place where the forces of darkness and light will meet in the open, either to come back into balance or end this world. Your partnership will be strong and you will take care of each other, but never forget you defend her most effectively by surrounding her only with thoughts of power and courage and safety."

"Will she be coming here?" asked Sasha. Will I meet her soon?" Ariel shook her head. "I know this is hard to understand, but it is extremely important. There is no 'soon', there is only 'now'. If you are to travel safely, you must remember that time is not linear, it is only a way of arranging experiences here on this earth. It is yours to command and it is critical you do so. That is the second lesson of the sunflower. Time belongs to you; you do not live in time."

Sasha had an idea. "Then I could go back in time and tell her what I know. It would make it easier for her. Maybe she wouldn't even close her heart." "You could," said Ariel gravely, "but what Traveler told you was right. If you do interfere, you will stunt her growth and she may never discover her purpose or remember her source. Each person must walk their own path, no matter how difficult it is for those who love them to watch."

Sasha's chin sagged. "Then what is the use of traveling in time?" Ariel looked irritated at that question. "It taught you the power carried in the thoughts you choose, didn't it? Traveler uses it when he 'turns' in flight, taking you both to other dimensions and other times. You can always use it to defend yourself if needed, or to hide or to shorten your journey in the eyes of those who believe time is real. Any other uses you will have to discover for yourself. That's enough for today." Ariel stomped off in a huff, tossing her great mane of yellow-brown hair, just as Gene and Traveler returned.

"She's in a temper," said Gene. "What happened?" Sasha looked sheepish. "I asked a pretty stupid question." Gene patted her affectionately. "Well, she didn't bat you across the garden so it can't be too bad. Don't worry about it. Her temper fits pass as suddenly as they come on. We'll have a nice evening together, and tomorrow the two of you must be on your way to continue your work. You two stirred up quite a ruckus in the energy fields of the earth, but it has settled down pretty well now and you should be able to make some great progress."

In the morning, Ariel sent Traveler and Sasha on their way with a cheerful wave from the porch, just before stretching back into the shape of a great lion. There was a lovely spot in the sun next to the pond. It was calling sweetly. “Come, have a nap.”

Friendship

To believe in the things you can see and touch is no belief at all. But to believe in the unseen is both a triumph and a blessing.

Bob Proctor

Beauty spent time in nature, by lakes and in the woods, as often as she could. When joy began to fade in her daily routine, she went looking for a dragonfly, inviting it to light on her. The delightful jolt was always there, and she thanked dragonfly profoundly for its help. She would sit quietly for hours, listening and watching and extending her essence. Hawks took their rest in the trees around her. Once she spotted an eagle.

She thought about the beautiful wolf and longed to see it and touch it; not just in a dream but in her waking life. Once she tried to call Helper and Comfort and Shadow, and thought for a second she could hear faint giggles. "I wish I hadn't closed them out of my heart and sent them away. I miss them all so much." She was amazed at how she could experience profound regret at losing her companions, and at the same time abiding joy for the memories she carried of them.

Today she needed the dragonfly desperately. She ached with missing Bones and couldn't shake the terrible grief. She walked to a favorite spot and sat on a warm rock with her feet dangling in the lake water. She slipped into the reverie that allowed her to reach out around her. She heard a PSSSSSS. PSSSSS. Not a happy sound. A water moccasin swam inches from her feet. Swallowing fear and opening her heart, a connection was made. "You are sitting in front of my nest. I can't get in." Eyes wide, Beauty answered, "I'll move right now, and I'll be very careful so I don't harm your nest. Forgive me, I didn't mean any disrespect." SSSSSSS. The snakes reply was soft. "Thank you. I will respect you as well, daughter of the earth."

Beauty's heart was pounding with excitement. "It's back! I can speak my special language again! Bones, where are you? We can talk now." Of course he was gone so there was no reply. Then her eyes widened with amazement as she realized the great gift Bones had given her. He had come to her, wiggled into her heart, and in his leaving had given her back her voice. When she poured all of herself into her last call for him, it had broken the last barrier to the return of her special language. Her voice rocketed through the earth. "Bones, I know you can hear me somewhere. Thank you! I love you!"

Margie called and the two of them went out for dinner that evening. "This is my treat", said Margie. "I can never thank you enough for what you did for me last year. Your wisdom was exactly what I needed to regain my perspective and my hope. You helped me break free from believing I had lost everything, and now my life is so rich and full! My new business is thriving and it's so much fun! I'm arranging custom adventures in sacred places. Some are for groups and some for individuals. I'm making lots of money, and bringing paying students to wonderful teachers who are great at what they teach, but don't have the business sense to find students. Everybody benefits. For me, the best part is all the amazing new friends I am meeting. I want to share it with you, Beauty. In fact I want to invite you to come along as my guest for a weekend. Please say you'll come."

"It sounds intriguing," said Beauty, "but what sort of spiritual adventures are you talking about?" "Anything you want," was the reply. "Some ask to learn about spiritual healing, or past life information, or a mystical experience, or communing with nature or animals. Some seek a spiritual discipline, or physical training that raises their vibration, or using their minds to create the life they want. I just put the word out and the right teacher always shows up. And I'm discovering some amazing places on our lovely earth; places that seem to quiver with aliveness and can change you just by spending time there. So, what do you want? Let me help you find it."

Beauty thought for a moment, and suddenly she was twelve years old again. She remembered helping the neighborhood priest weave the shining strands, and how the priests seemed to be protected from the big darkness. She remembered her longing to weave shining strands freely and use her special language without fear; how it felt so right to be able to do that. "Can you find someone who will teach me how to be a priest?" Margie looked startled. "You mean, like, a Catholic priest?" "Well, no. Not exactly." Beauty sighed. How much could she tell Margie? She decided on a short version.

"When I was a kid, I could do things that most people couldn't. Sometimes frightening things would happen to me when certain others noticed what I was doing. I learned some priests could do some of what I did, but they stayed safe, so I asked one of them to help me become a priest. You can imagine his reaction. Sin of pride, trafficking with Satan, all that sort of stuff. That pretty well crushed my spirit when I was twelve. For me today, learning to be a 'priest' means learning to use all the innate stuff that wells up in me, safely and without fear. I know it all has a purpose, or it wouldn't be there, and I know that purpose has to be good. I just don't know what it is."

Then Beauty took a real risk with her friend. "Margie, my family gave me the name 'Beauty', but it's not my true name. I must discover my purpose in order to find my true name, and I can't do that unless I learn the skills that keep the priests safe when they use their real powers."

Margie shook her head, then grinned. "I should have known you wouldn't be just another spiritual geek looking for a happy trip. OK, I'll get the word out and we'll see what kind of master teacher shows up for you. By the way, what I think you left unsaid in your story is that you work with light energy. That's what puts you in danger. I'm not sure what that means. It's just something I hear a lot from the people I work with. Maybe one of these days I'll have to arrange my own spiritual adventure. Meanwhile, lets finish this bottle of wine and talk about our fall wardrobes. In my opinion, what you need more than anything is to lighten up and just play. I don't need any master teachers to help you with that."

The two women finished the evening with warm laughter and silly stories. They planned a shopping trip for pretty play clothes. Beauty went home feeling lighter than since she was a kid. Margie had returned the favor of a year ago, and offered her new hope and a bright outlook. She hoped she could keep this new friend for life and not have to leave her behind.

Back to the Garden

Dreaming is an act of pure imagination, attesting in all men a creative power, which, if it were available in waking, would make every man a Dante or a Shakespeare.

H. F. Hedge

Running errands one day soon after, Beauty ran head on into a large woman wearing loose, flowing clothing. She was no age and all ages, haughty and humble, strangely dressed but no one noticed. "So sorry," Beauty said. "Clumsy of me." "Not at all, the woman answered. "What can I do for you?" "Do for me? What do you mean?" The woman's eyes were intense. "You called for my help. Something about becoming a priest." Beauty blinked and backed away nervously. "But you're a woman." Looking offended, the woman said, "Who do you think teaches the priests?" "Well, seminaries…. Other priests…… none of them are women." "Hah! Your eyes deceive you, Beauty. You see what you expect, not what is really here. Look again."

The air shimmered and there was no woman, just a fleeting image of St Francis. Then a large goose took flight from where she had been standing. Beauty whirled in confusion, certain the woman had just stepped away quickly, but there was no sign of her. The sidewalk wasn't crowded so there was nowhere to hide. "Where did she get the idea about priests, and how did she know my name?" The old fear of being caught by the darkness made her shiver and she hurried on her way. She finished her shopping and had her teeth cleaned, looking nervously over her shoulder for someone following her.

When she got home later that day, a goose was waiting at her front door. She walked past her house and dropped in on a neighbor, hoping the goose would leave. It waited. She used the neighbor's phone and called Margie. "What are you up to? Did you send them?" "What are you talking about?" asked Margie. "Send who?" "A large woman talking about priest training. I ran into her on the street and she knew my request and my name. And there is a goose that showed up when she disappeared and it's now sitting at my front door. It won't leave and I'm afraid to go home. I'm calling from a neighbor's house."

"Let's see, a woman who disappears and a goose tracking you. Did you have some really strong coffee this morning? Do you have a fever?" "Margie, don't mock me. This is too scary. You said you were going to look for a teacher for me and this woman shows up acting like she can teach me to be a priest. I thought you sent her." "That's not how it works," said Margie. "I find the right teacher, then we travel to where they are. I don't just send you someone. Who else have you talked to? You have some pretty 'out there' friends. Have you told any of them what you told me?" "No one," insisted Beauty. "I haven't told anyone my story since the priest got so angry with me years ago."

"I have an idea," mused Margie. "Remember how defeated I was at the ending of my marriage? Then you led me in that visualization and we danced to that song.

Something in me shifted. In a few days my whole world shifted. I was getting lots of ideas and people were just showing up with opportunities. Has something shifted in you recently? Something that breaks down barriers and lets in new ideas and new people? Maybe there are teachers all around you and they've been waiting for you to open your mind to them."

"Yes!" cried Beauty. "But not my mind, it's my heart that had to open. Mr. Sam Bones helped me crack the last wall. Thanks so much Margie. I've got to go." "Wait a minute, where are you going? What are you doing now?" "I need to go talk to a goose," was the excited reply.

Beauty grabbed her purchases, thanked her neighbor and headed home, excitement filling her. The goose was still at her front door, snoozing with its head under one wing. It woke up as she approached and shook out its feathers. She opened the door, put down her packages, and moving deep into her cells sent a feeling of welcome. "Won't you come in?" she asked, in her special language. "Actually, I came to invite you to take a trip with me," replied the goose. "If you're ready to start your training, that is. It'll be lots of fun, I promise. We'll go to some wonderful places and I'll introduce you to my friends and they will help you discover your purpose."

Her eyes wide, Beauty asked how long they would be gone. "Hard to say. One thing leads to another opportunity, and synchronicity is important. Once you start walking on the circle of life, anything can happen. It's a wonderful adventure," replied the goose. Beauty could feel his yearning for her to come. "But I have a job, and this house. I can't just pick up and leave. I need to arrange vacation time and find someone to take care of things, and I really need to know how long we'll be gone."

The goose considered the best way to tell her, then just blurted it all out. "I can fix it so no one even notices you're gone. Time, as you understand it, isn't the way it works in other where's and other when's. Beauty, time is not your master. You are free to master it!"

Her amazement growing, Beauty said, "are you sure? We can leave and be gone for days and days, then come back and only minutes will have passed?" "Better than that" said the grinning goose. "We can come back in almost the same instant. The only think I can't do is take you backward in your time. Not that I think it can't be done, I just haven't learned how yet. Actually, I'm pretty sure I could learn it if I chose. It must be a lot like taking 'turns' when I travel. But that doesn't matter. The important thing is you can travel with me and never miss a step in this where/when, and you will remember everything from both spaces."

A shiver of fear passed through her as she wondered if the darkness had sent this bird to get her. She strained to feel the heart of the goose.

She found mischief, a sense of adventure, loyalty, self assurance, and most of all, kindness. The goose preened a feather. "Good for you, Beauty. It's important to check the heart of those around you. You just need to learn how to shield yourself when you do that and keep yourself hidden, in case you are listening in to some unsavory character. No point in inviting trouble. So, can we go now?"

A great YES surged through Beauty. "How shall we travel?" "Hop on. We're going to fly." But you're too small to carry me," she protested. "Your eyes are as inaccurate as your sense of time. You are only seeing what you expect to see. Trust me, and hop on." Hearing the words of the large woman repeated was another assurance that this was ‘right’. “OK, but who am I flying with? What’s your name?” she asked. “Traveler,” was the answer. “Is that your true name? The name that tells your purpose?

Her excitement was rising. “Yes it is, now hop on and lets go flying.” She obeyed, and a shudder passed through her as she mounted Traveler. Either the bird had shape shifted or she had, and she was lifted on powerful wings which quickly left everything familiar behind.

They flew away from her town and crossed hills and valleys, streams and lakes. Beauty was entranced by the sight of the sunset from so high up. Then the stars appeared and their rich beauty, the thick, gleaming clouds of them took her breath away. She was getting tired, and thought Traveler must be really worn out. He was doing all the work. Just as she had that thought, Traveler circled into a low clearing. There was a pond with a grassy bank and a small hut nearby. “I’m going to have a bit to eat and a drink,” said Traveler. See what you can find in that hut. It’s quite safe.” “Are you sure it’s safe?” asked Beauty. “Use your heart and check for yourself,” was the answer. “You need the practice.” Beauty sent her awareness around and into the hut. Except for the low hum of some insects, all was quiet.

She went inside and rummaged around. There was a small camp stove with a gas cylinder attached. She found some canned soup and a pot, and managed to get the stove going and the soup hot. She opened a package of crackers, mouth watering with hunger. It was a great meal. She took the pot and her spoon outside to wash it with sand and pond water, then returned everything the way she found it, whispering a silent ‘thank you’ for whoever had left the soup. Traveler had finished his meal and his bath. “Time for some sleep. I’ll be over there in that bush till morning." "But, can't you sleep inside with me? I'm a bit scared."

"I could," replied the bird, "but it would be a very uncomfortable night for me. You'll be fine in there."

She sighed and went back in the hut. There was a can of meat, more crackers and a can of peaches. She decided that would be her breakfast and set them out for morning. She found a clean towel and went back out to the pond and washed her face, and tried scrubbing her teeth with her finger. Finally she gave in to spending the night alone in the hut.

There was a small cot in one corner. The blanket looked clean, but she took it outside and gave it a good shake anyway. She lay down, feeling nervous about sleeping in this strange place, wondering if Traveler knew any great orb weaver spiders or perhaps a marvelous wolf. Tiredness won and she curled up, punched the pillow, and slept immediately.

~~~~~~~~~~~~~~~~

Beauty was driving fast on the rutted forest road. She needed time alone so badly. The man she lived with had been cruel again, hurling hurtful words at her most sensitive insecurities. She brought very little with her, planning to spend several days alone examining her life and searching for what she might do to find peace. His parting words as she ran out of the house were, "You selfish witch! Running off to do what you want to do. Who's going to fix my dinner? What am I supposed to do by myself?" She shuddered at the memory. Why couldn't she find a relationship with at least some kindness, if not love?

The cabin stood alone near a pond with a grassy bank. It was rustic, but sturdy. She carried in her few supplies in
~~~~~~~~~~~~~~~~

one trip, then went back to her car for her one extravagance; flowers. She had brought a huge bouquet with her, hoping their beauty and scent would ease her aching heart and confused soul. She arranged them in an old stone jug, and placed them where she could see them from anywhere in the room. There was a large, rustic chair in one corner, and a simple bed in another. It had crisscrossed ropes for springs and a huge featherbed on top. There was a big fireplace, with a trestle table and two chairs in front of it. Two windows and an open door let in the light of the setting sun. She busied herself for a little while carrying in wood, stacking it neatly, and getting a fire going.

"What on earth am I going to do here for a week?" she thought to herself. "No books, no radio, just my own miserable thoughts. I must have been nuts to come here like this." She sighed and drummed her fingers on the table, thinking about packing up and going home. But she wouldn't do that. She would not let *him* see her give up after making such a stink about how she needed to get away alone.

She glanced at the open door and to her horror saw a huge bear sauntering in. He reared up on his hind legs as he approached her. His teeth were long and yellow, and dripped saliva as he snarled at her. The claws on his front paws were long and black, glinting in the firelight. Her heart pounding with terror, she glanced around desperately for a place to hide, but it was just a small, one room cabin. The bear came closer, sniffing and tossing its head, owning the place. Beauty searched the room again, not moving anything but her head and her eyes. A dash for the door would take her within inches of the bear. She would never make it. She noticed a large gun hanging above the fireplace. Her eyes also caught sight of a crock of honey in the middle of the table.

"Grab the gun," she screamed internally. "It's your only hope. Grab the gun and shoot. You can't miss from this close." A part of her self argued with her. "That bear is faster than you. You move and he'll be on you before you can reach the gun. Hold still! Pray!! Maybe he'll leave." Then another voice spoke. "Give him the honey." The internal dialogue heated up. "ARE YOU NUTS? Grab the gun and shoot!" "No, no! Hold very still and pray." "Give him the honey."

At war with herself, she stared at the bear. He stared back, then moved his head slightly closer. Something snapped in Beauty, and trembling, she reached for the crock of honey and held it out toward the bear, all the while screaming on the inside, "you're crazy, you're going to die right now!" Summoning her last scrap of courage, she cautiously set the honey on the floor in front of the bear, then inched backward, still glancing nervously at the gun. The bear picked up the honey, dipped one paw into it, and licked. He continued until the crock was empty, then carefully licked away every drop from his long, sharp claws.

The bear began to glow and change shape, becoming a larger than life human-like form made of radiating white light. A beautiful, melodic voice said, "because you have fed me, you shall never be hungry again." Beauty's fear disappeared as the figure embraced her, and faded away. Her heart surged with a knowing she couldn't put into words. It felt as though she was connected to a very deep well of something precious. She reached out to close the door of the cottage, and woke up on the narrow cot, in the bright morning sunlight of the little hut.

She woke slowly and gently, rolling the memory of the dream around in her mind with wonder and the oddest sense of peace. She stretched, got up and ate the peaches with some crackers, then went looking for Traveler. He was frolicking in the pond, ready to start the day. "Traveler, what do you know about bears?" "Not much," said the goose. "I haven't actually met one, and I'm not in any hurry, considering their size and fierce reputation. Why do you ask?" Beauty told him her dream in all its detail, and how clear and vivid it remained in her mind. Traveler looked at her very seriously. "That wasn't just a dream. It was part of your Spirit Journey. Pay attention and examine every detail. There will be many messages for you in that dream. When you find your next teacher, be sure to ask about it."

Beauty had not thought of Spirit Journey in years, and the words seemed to wake something in her; a longing for something or someone, a sense of excited anticipation. "This must be part of discovering my true name and my purpose," she thought. Suddenly anxious to continue their way, she called, "Hey Traveler, are you ready to go?" "Hop on," was the response. She felt the same shudder as she approached the goose and shifted a dimension to get on his back. Traveler circled upward till they were high above the trees, then flew straight for the horizon.

By late morning Traveler was circling for a landing. They arrived in a garden overflowing with a riot of flowers. Sundials and little statues were tucked among the blooms or perched on stones. Ho Tai grinned from a fence corner, Quan Yin presided over a bowl of impatiens and St Francis guarded a bowl of cracked corn near a tree. Chipmunks and squirrels chattered at each other as they competed for the corn. One end of a bench was held up by a stone likeness of Bacchus and a whimsical crane made of scrap iron and stone presided over a sparkling pond. Beauty drank in the color and shapes, the intoxicating scent and she longed to spend hours daydreaming in this magical place. They walked toward a small house with spreading porches and wind chimes hanging from the corners.

"Hello there," came a gravelly voice. A small, old man sat cross legged on a cushion. "Welcome to the garden. Do you like it?" It's amazing," replied Beauty. "If it were mine, I'd never want to leave." Traveler spoke up. "Hey, Gene, good to see you again. Are you here on a visit or is this a working trip?" "Working, always working these days." The old man rose grinning, moving closer to greet Traveler, and his skinny frame revealed a wiry strength. The two circled in an awkward dance; knees, elbows and wings flapping. Gene laughed and Traveler squawked. Beauty stared. They settled on the porch together to catch up, their news sprinkled with reminiscences.

Since she was not part of the conversation, Beauty wandered off and allowed herself the luxury of sinking into the full presence of the garden.

As she had learned the past couple of years, the more she relaxed, the more acutely aware of the hum of life she became. She found a bench next to a tiny pond and sat, closing her eyes. It felt as though her essence was melting into a golden pool of light. Every sound; birds, insects, rustling leaves, flowing sap, was part of a symphony she could hear and see and feel in her body, and her own breath became part of the great song. She felt a Presence come near, and when she opened her eyes it was no surprise to see the tall woman she had bumped into a few days ago standing near her.

"So, are you still seeking to know the powers of priest-hood," asked the woman. "Yes," was the answer. "Hmmm. Do you still see me as a woman?" "Well, of course," Beauty replied. "You are still only looking at what you expect to see. Look again." Beauty barely blinked and where the woman had stood there was now a lion, its great shaggy head unmistakably carrying the essence of the woman. The conversation continued in the language that made Beauty's heart sing. "My name is Ariel. Welcome to my home. If you are willing to examine everything you think is true, I am willing to begin teaching you."

"Oh, yes!' exclaimed Beauty. "I'll do anything." The sun turned a strange color and a chill blew through the air. "Don't say that!" bellowed the lion. "You are inviting difficulty and unexpected consequences along with learning and I don't need those in my garden. The lion roared, turning in all directions. The sun returned to normal and the air warmed. "Just tell me if you are willing to learn and change some beliefs." "I'm willing to learn. I'm willing to change my beliefs," said the shaken Beauty. For a second she had felt ice grip her heart and her vision had darkened strangely. "Then pick yourself a flower and let's go to the house. Your first teacher is waiting there," invited the lion. Beauty bent to choose a flower and when she straightened the woman was standing next to her. "By the way my dear, I am Ariel in any form you see me." Beauty had no need to ask if that was her true name, but she did have a question. "Ariel, why is it when you're in lion form, you are a male, but in human form you are female?"

Ariel grinned. "I like it when students notice subtleties. It means they are paying attention. Most people would have been so frightened by a lion they would have missed it. Dear child, everyone shares masculine and feminine natures. I have simply learned to shape shift them in one body. Useful sometimes."

As they approached the porch, Gene and Traveler were discussing the imbalance of light and dark and how much there was to do if harmony was to be restored. Gene nodded as he watched Beauty approach. "Looks like she's ready to learn. Been tough on her, I'll bet." He seemed able to read her memories along with her spirit. “Still she’s one tough cookie. Just as well for her. She didn’t break.” Traveler listened to Gene’s musings with interest. He really didn’t know anything about Beauty, just that he was asked to go get her, and that he had come to like her.

“Beauty and Gene, you’ll be working together for a while,” commanded Ariel as she reached the porch. “But, could I ask a question first?” pleaded Beauty. Ariel nodded, picking up a bell from a side table and ringing it vigorously. Lunch was brought, along with cool, fresh water. “Tell us your story first,” said Gene. It may help us answer your questions more clearly.” Beauty took a deep breath, gathering her courage. She had not told her whole story to anyone since the priest in her parish had thrown her out of his office when she was twelve. Now the story was longer and more complex. Would they believe her? She didn’t think she could bear it if they got angry and told her to leave. There was nowhere else to go except back to a quiet life, hiding from the big darkness. After the last 24 hours, that would be unbearable. Crossing her arms tightly across her chest, she once again poured out her heart, including every detail she remembered.

They stopped her for questions, particularly when she told about weaving the silver strands with the priest in the procession. Ariel bent forward, listening intently. Gene jumped up and stomped about the porch with his back turned when she told about being condemned as a sinner who was trafficking with the devil. When she described the wooden feeling that came over her, then the rage that caused her to shut her heart to everyone, Gene hit the side of the house with his fist. Ariel looked at him and said in a surprisingly gentle voice, “Gene we all have our trials. She got through it. She’s going to be fine now.”

Beauty continued, and when she told about Bones and her last anguished call for him, Gene leaped up again, but this time he might have been cheering a great victory as he shouted "YES!", fist punching the air this time. "I knew he could do it! He is one great bone cruncher, that one!" "What are you talking about? Do you know him? Where is he? Can I see him? Is he OK?" Questions poured out of her as she frantically looked around, hoping to see the white cat walking toward her. "Do you know what he did for you?" asked Ariel. "Yes, he gave me my voice back. The special language I had forgotten returned." "Of course, of course, but do you understand why?" persisted Ariel. "No, I see you don't. You must embrace the foundation, the very bones of all your pain before you can transform your pain into your great strength. Bones sat with you and loved you until you told him your story, finally accepting and embracing all the memories and all the hurts. That's why your voice came back, and now you will find it has more power than ever."

Beauty was crying softly. "You all seem to know him. Is he here? "No," answered Ariel. "Bones doesn't live in this dimension. In fact he doesn't much like to visit it. It's not easy being the crusher of pain. He can feel what he helps others release when he's in physical form, so he avoids it when he can. What is here for you is his love. Bones only acts when he loves, and he loves you." Beauty's face was in her hands. "I wouldn't have him suffer for anything. I just miss him so much. The loneliness is worst of all. Worse than the fear, worse than all the struggles. There seems to be no way to ease it."

Ariel reached above her head, snapping her fingers. Her hand disappeared momentarily, as though it had passed through a curtain. When she pulled it back down, a beautiful fragrance settled over the porch. Beauty's head shot up just as Ariel handed her a perfect lavender rose. "You are no longer alone," whispered Ariel. "Whatever you face in the rest of your days, the loneliness is over.

Different companions and helpers may come and go, but as long as you keep your heart open, you will always be filled with the love of those around you."

Beauty smiled at her gratefully, blew her nose, placed the rose in the remnants of her glass of water and continued her story. When she finished with yesterday's bear dream, Gene jumped up again, doing an awkward, ecstatic dance. "Holy Moley! This is so fine! This is so, so fine!" His whacky behavior got them all laughing. Ariel got up and stretched, catlike. "Beauty, what is your question?"

"When we first met, you said I wanted to train for the priesthood. That's not quite right. What I want is to learn what they know so I can use my special language and weave patterns with silver threads without being caught and attacked by the big darkness. The priests who can weave don't seem to get attacked, and I want that so much. You implied that priests were not trained in seminaries or by other priests, but by women. What did you mean? There are seminaries all over the world and no one ever heard of a woman being in one, let alone teaching there."

"It's complicated," sighed Ariel. "I'm going to keep this as simple as I can for now. Seminaries do not turn people into priests, they simply train those who are priests how to behave according to whatever authority is in power in a given reality. True priests tend to be a rowdy bunch, following the call of their own inner spirit no matter what. In this dimension, priesthood exists in a hierarchical structure, and those in power create seminaries that primarily teach priests to surrender to their earthly superiors and be obedient. The priest who rejected you probably believed he was telling you to surrender to God, but he was really telling you to submit to the hierarchy ruling his world.

"Priesthood is not bestowed by anyone. Priesthood is a soul pattern, an energy force carried by certain beings. Its source is more ancient than any existing scripture, and the identity of the first teachers is lost in antiquity but we know they were not exclusively men or women because priests were not exclusively men or women. That's only a recent aberration, and one that is not shared by all humans. Once a person has accepted the patterning of 'priest' on their soul, it stays forever, across all dimensions and times, unless the individual knowingly rejects it for something else or abuses it. Priests in this dimension who carry the power you seek were not trained in it by any seminary. The ones who can still use it carry the power as a soul memory."

Ariel looked deeply at Beauty. "You carry that soul patterning. So do I. The only thing you need is help in remembering how to use it. The bear in your dream gave you a truth coming from ancient wisdom and forgotten today. "Because you have fed me, you will never be hungry again." When the world is in balance, all beings feed and nurture each other. It is time now, in your Spirit Journey, to begin to awaken and remember. So, are you willing?"

Beauty caught herself before the longing rising in her caused her to say she'd do anything. "I'm willing!" she answered. "Good. Do you want to hang on to that rose a bit longer, or are you feeling comforted?" asked Ariel. "It's OK, you can put it back now, but how did you know where to find it?" "I'm the one who sent you Shadow and the other two, ….and don't start with the questions," Ariel insisted, as she saw Beauty's eyes widen. The gentleness was gone and her commanding presence was back in full force. "We'll get to more questions later. Now it's time to get to work. Gene! She thinks what she sees with her eyes is real. Can you help this poor thing?"

Remembering

Hope is the thing with feathers that perches in the soul, and sings the tunes without the words and never stops at all.

Emily Dickinson

With a typical jerky motion, Gene jumped up. "Come on gal, let's see what we can do about your sight. You must have some, somewhere, priest and all." They left the porch together walking past flower beds and finally a vegetable patch. Gene squinted. "What do you see ahead of us?" he asked. "A picket fence," was the answer. "A rather pretty picket fence. I particularly like it because it's not painted white or anything; it's just natural wood." Gene squinted again, this time directly into her eyes, inches away. "Hmph! Let's move up for a closer look. If you are willing to give up the idea that this is a fence, look again. This time don't look at the fence, look through it or past it, allowing your eyes to go soft, feeling with all your senses while you look. "

Beauty rebelled. "I don't think I know how to do that. In fact I'm sure I don't. It just doesn't make any sense." Gene's hands were on his hips, head jutting forward on his neck. "Quittin' already are you? Look, *nothing* happens until you decide. Make up your mind you're going to do it, then just do it." The word 'quittin' stung her and she decided. Beauty lifted her chin, made a face, and whirled back to the fence, but she did it her way. Instead of softening her eyes and relaxing, she squinted them the way Gene had and let her annoyance rule. The fence wavered in the sunshine and suddenly she saw a wall of round, ugly little faces with pointy, sharp teeth. Their mouths were opened as though they were about to screech or bite. She jumped back and grabbed Gene's arm. "Yikes, what's that?" she squealed. She didn't like the answer. "That's your energy," said Gene. "That's what it looks like when you're feeling angry and vengeful." She was shocked into silence, so he continued. "It looks ugly and frightening, and it can be very dangerous. Those mouths and teeth have terrifying screeches and bites, but remember the anger is not evil. How you use it determines its worth. You can use it to harm willfully, or it can motivate you to action that can save your life or the lives of others. Anger, tempered by wisdom, can be a valuable tool."

Gene leaned back against the fence that wasn't a fence, picked a long blade of grass to chew and invited her to try again, this time following his instructions. He looked nonchalant, thumbs in his jeans pockets, but his eyes sharply caught every detail. Beauty did as he said, letting her eyes soften out of focus and relaxing as she extended her awareness. It took three attempts, but finally the fence wavered in the sun again, this time changing into a misty fog. Occasionally a wraith like owl shape would fly past. "What is it?" she whispered. "It's a camouflage shield. No one can see this house and garden unless Ariel wants them to. The owls fly keeping watch. They will tell us if danger approaches. Let me tell you, your anger energy put a ripple in the shield that jolted Ariel till she figured out what it was." Beauty blushed at that, not willing yet to explore the larger implications of her energy pattern.

"Would you like to try again?" asked Gene. "Clear your mind of everything you think you have seen and check it out." Beauty tried again. This time it was very easy. The fence was still there, but instead of empty fields surrounding the house, she saw a small town neighborhood, much like the ones where she had once lived. There were houses nearby with people and kids and dogs and all sorts of busyness. She turned to Gene, confusion on her face.

"So, what am I seeing now? This at least looks normal but I don't know what to believe." Gene nodded, smiling, then looked very serious. "Young woman, those are people out there. They are children of the earth, living their lives in ordinary ways. This house and garden is in the middle of their neighborhood and they believe they see a fence and a garden and a house with a big porch. They believe Ariel is a retired teacher or doctor or something. There's a lot of speculation because few of them have actually met her, but they have decided anyone with a garden this lovely must be trustworthy."

"They *believe* they see all this?" stammered Beauty, waving her hand toward Ariel's property. "What do you mean 'they believe'? Is it all an illusion? Isn't it real at all?" "What do you believe?" asked Gene, with a wink. Beauty groaned in confusion. "Why are you twisting things like this? Is this place real or isn't it?" "Are you real?" was the response. "What!" squealed Beauty. Gene nearly cackled. "Is this woman standing before me, the one with dark hair and dark eyes and a fine tan on her skin, real? Or is this just a vision created for my benefit so we can share the Spirit Journey chosen by the eternal soul that is her true self?"

It was too much. Beauty dropped to the ground with a thump, her face blank and her mind reeling. The energy of her essence was whirling around her in a flashing, multicolored spiral. Gene moved his hand over the fence, and only the empty field remained in sight. He bent toward her and offered his hand. "Come on gal, that's a lot for one day. Let's go see if Ariel has anything to eat." She got up and they walked to the house in silence. She would shake her head from time to time, as if to rid it of some bit of insanity.

Gene and Ariel kept up a lively conversation over dinner, but Beauty toyed with her food and didn't speak. As the sun was setting, she noticed Traveler was nowhere in sight. "It's probably time for Traveler and I to leave. Where is he?" "Oh, my dear I thought you knew," said Ariel. "Traveler has been called to another assignment. He said to give you his love and he would be back for you when you are finished. You are to stay here for a while."

"But what if I don't want to? What if I want to leave and go home? I do in fact. I want to go home now." Ariel touched her hand gently. "Of course you are free to leave if you wish, but only Traveler can take you back to your home. He is expecting to come back for you as soon as you have finished what you came here to learn. If you leave, he may not know where to find you. We have prepared a room here for you. It is yours if you want it. No one will force you, but you are very welcome." Beauty dissolved in tears. "Then may I please go to bed now? Please?"

She was shown to a lovely, airy room with its own tiny deck overlooking the garden. Cool water waited in a small crystal pitcher with a matching glass. A vase of flowers was on the dresser, and a closet contained a change of clothes. They looked much like the flowing robes Ariel wore. She sighed, thinking wistfully of her favorite jeans. The tears had stopped, but she was feeling a sadness so intense her throat ached and there was a dull pain in her solar plexus. She curled up on the bed, arms wrapped tightly around her middle, as if to keep it from breaking open. Sleep eluded her for hours. Her mind raced with memories as she tossed on the bed. If only she hadn't closed her heart and run away all those years ago. Her last thought as she finally drifted off to sleep was the memory of emerging into the white tiled hospital room.

Millions of stars pulsed on the backdrop of the velvet black sky, so thick in places they looked like gleaming clouds. She looked down at the human form sleeping on a wad of tortured sheets, startled to realize the form belonged to her. The memories of the Spirit Journey taken in this body integrated into her soul, and she remembered and understood everything. The fear, the loneliness, the sadness all drained from her as she reviewed all that had happened and all she had learned during this earth journey. The greatest learning of all, beyond any other wisdom, was to keep her heart open. She could see how cutting herself off from pain and fear had also cut her off from experiencing love. She looked back at the sleeping form with compassion and made a promise. "You will never again be without love."

She began to expand her essence; tendrils of energy curling out from her and reaching through space and time. A very powerful force was pulling at her, and she had no desire to resist. Something curled itself around and through her, bringing such warmth and peace, such belonging. Then with a gasp of joy, memories flooded in and she knew. MOTHER! She floated in a whirling sea of delicious scent and sound and sensation. Light thrilled her whole being as it pierced her and melted into her essence. Then the Communion with Mother began, and all she had forgotten about the Spirit Journey she had agreed to take flooded into her memory. All is well. She had not made mistakes, only engaged in earthbound learning, which was part of the Journey. She saw that everything she learned was now a part of the energy patterns of the earth, available to all who lived there.

In a communion of pure knowing, she reviewed her Spirit Journey with Mother. Her companions had been true and were still waiting for her. Those she had not yet found were beginning to sense her approach. It would take all of them to bring the forces of light and dark back into balance. She understood that the wholeness she felt in the presence of Mother was often masked from a physical body. Only a few could touch it, and only sometimes. She also understood the struggles of being human were never punishment, only urgings to learn and grow and maintain balance in the forces of the earth. The only thing that caused suffering was resistance to the flow of life. When balance is restored, resistance dissolves and humans take another step on their evolutionary path.

She had to know one more thing. "This person I became missed you so desperately and was confused and lost when the memory of Spirit Journey faded. When I go back this time, will I remember all of this? Will I be able to remember you?" The reply was gentle. "You will have a clear sense of purpose that will strengthen you, and teachers who will remind you of the need to balance life's forces. You will not remember me as you know me in this moment, but you will feel my nearness as a power moving through you. Your suffering is over, dear child. The full richness of human life is yours now, and your Spirit will rejoice as it expands through what you experience. Now, it's time to go back. Your companions wait."

Beauty woke slowly and gently. Someone had come in during the night and removed her shoes, straightened the bed, and covered her with a light sheet. The remnants of a dream tickled her memory. She strained to capture it then noticed a sense of peace and certainty filling her heart. She knew she had a Spirit Journey and a purpose, and she was ready now. Stretching, she rolled out of bed and found her own bath behind a closed door. She dressed in the new clothes, feeling a bit odd at the length and fullness, but she wouldn't complain.

The household was still asleep so she wandered into the garden. The dew of night time kissed soft petals and sparkled in the early sunshine. Slipping into a familiar reverie, she allowed the rhythm and pulse of flowers and insects to nourish her. "Ahh!" she realized. "Touching the essence of living creatures like this is not unlike seeing that fence yesterday in different ways." She looked at her own hand and watched it waver and reform according to her thoughts. Then she experimented with a butterfly, giggling as it disappeared and reappeared. She understood she was not changing the butterfly, only her own interaction with it. That was comforting. It meant she didn't need to be afraid of causing harm.

A silver bell tinkled. Ariel stood on the porch, waving. The smell of bacon drifted in on the breeze and Beauty's mouth watered. She was certain she was hungry enough for both dinner and breakfast. As she stepped on the porch, Ariel inspected her closely, and the worry lines between her eyes smoothed as she saw the peace in Beauty's face and the power in her demeanor. "I see you slept well," commented the tall woman, "and you look like you're ready to continue your lessons." Beauty laughed. "After breakfast, please! And my thanks to whoever covered me and pulled off my shoes." Breakfast appeared just as Gene wandered in, yawning. Beauty talked about experimenting with her hand and the butterfly in the garden. "Is it true that I am only shifting my perception and can't do any harm?" she asked.

Ariel answered carefully. "It is true in this case, but there are many other ways of using your energy. That is what you are here to learn. It is possible to harm or destroy a physical form, but you cannot do harm to the essence of another. Had you killed the butterfly, its essence would remain as potential for another of its kind. If you killed it carelessly or in cruelty, you would have harmed your own essence." The lessons of her spider friend returned and Beauty shared them with Ariel and Gene; all beings are children of the earth and deserve respect.

Understanding washed over her. "Human beings carelessly, usually unconsciously, killed other living beings all the time, harming their own spirits as they did. They tried to use darkness to hide their own shame, but this just turned darkness away from its true purpose of nurturing gestating life, and made it fearful and aggressive. This is how darkness got out of balance with light!" She shivered as she shared her ideas with her friends. Ariel's head snapped to attention. "Young woman, you have just demonstrated your true purpose. Do you understand what you just did?" "I just had an insight," replied Beauty. Gene winked over the top of his coffee cup. "It was much more than an insight. Let's see if we can stimulate more of it, so you can recognize it. Lets go, gal. Are you ready to learn?"

Beauty jumped up and tripped on the unaccustomed hem of the long gown. "Sorry," said Ariel. "It's all I had to give you. We'll have your jeans clean for tomorrow." "I'll be fine, as long as Gene doesn't get grumpy about me not moving fast enough. Let's go, skinny," she grinned. Her step was light and she moved with confidence into the new day of lessons. "OK, smart aleck. First answer this question. If you want something, how do you make it happen?" Beauty was quick to answer. "You get off your backside and do whatever needs to be done."

"Not so fast. What comes before that?" She thought a moment and remembered yesterday's lesson. "You have to decide." "Good!" said Gene, with an evil twitch on his upper lip. "Then, how do you make something you don't want happen?" Beauty scowled. "What do you mean? I don't *decide* to have bad things happen to me." The evil twitch repeated. "So, I suppose there are hateful forces out there just waiting to pounce on you, and there's nothing you can do about it. You are their victim and you are helpless. Is that what you mean? In fact, there are good forces out there just waiting to help you. You don't have any power there either. You just have to hang on and hope." Gene waited patiently as she sat on a bench and thought that one through.

Her answer came carefully and slowly. "I know I have a purpose; that my Spirit chose to be here now for a reason. That was my first decision and it generated a response from other sources, both positive and negative. The big darkness attacks me when it finds me because my choices oppose it, not because I'm helpless. Then I have made many other choices in my life. Some were good and some were foolish, and all carried consequences. The most important consequence from every choice is the opportunity to learn more and choose more wisely." Gene looked very satisfied, the evil twitch now replaced by a slow smile. Ariel watched the pair walk away, their voices growing fainter as they sparred with each other. She heaved a deep sigh of relief and lowered her head into her hands, whispering words of gratitude. The girl was going to make it. She was going to be just fine.

The two headed for the garden gate. "You have learned to use your energy to alter what you see. Now you will use your energy to alter an event. Use caution. It is important that you do no harm unless it is the only way to stop a death. Let's practice. Watch that bee." A honey bee was flying toward a flower. Gene tilted his head slightly and the bee stopped, then began flying in a circle the size of an apple, inches from the flower. Gene turned away and the bee settled on the flower. "Your turn," he said. "But find your own bee. We don't want to wear that one out."

Beauty slipped into a reverie, spotted a bee, then sent it a gentle message to come to her and circle. Nothing happened. She sharpened her focus and decided the bee would circle above her head, then sent out a commanding instruction. The bee turned in midflight and started flying above her head, round and round. She sent it gratitude before she released it to find a flower. It was energized, not tired like Gene's bee. "What did you do?" he asked. "Blessed it. Said thanks, that's all. My Grandma Mary taught me that." Gene looked thoughtful. "Well, as long as you're careful."

They walked through the garden gate together, into the village surrounding the house. People waved. They ducked down an alley and saw a poorly kept back yard. A man and woman were arguing loudly, faces red and arms waving. The man made a fist and punched her. A child ran out of the house screaming, "Daddy don't, please Daddy, don't hit Mommy. Please, please." His little hands grabbed the man's leg but he was easily shaken off. Beauty's anger boiled as she watched the brutality. The man outweighed his wife by at least a hundred pounds and was powerfully built. As she struggled to get up, he raised his arm again. "Careful," was Gene's fierce whisper, as he recognized Beauty's anger. "Do no harm."

Beauty firmly took control of her hot energy and spun a silver thread, tripping the man as he swung. He lunged to his feet yelling, "Woman you tripped me. How dare you trip me?" The woman dodged behind a tree, avoiding his wild swing and Beauty flung another silver thread at his ankles. He fell again, then looked confused as he realized his wife couldn't have tripped him. But his rage was out of control and he started for her again as she dashed for safety in the house. Beauty flung strand after strand, pinning his arms to his side and finally pulling him down and binding him to a tree. He howled once, the rage on his face melted, and confusion and fear set in. He couldn't see the silver strands because there couldn't be any such thing. They held him firmly, as Beauty and Gene slipped back through the gate into the garden.

Beauty was exultant. "That's the first time I've used the silver strands since I was a kid. I can still do it, Gene. I can still do it!" Gene shook his head in amazement. "I've never seen anything quite like that before. What exactly did you do?" Beauty had to think a bit to remember what Spider had taught her. "We all do it, but most people can't see it. My personal energy creates my life, and how I use intention to direct that energy determines the pattern I weave. I intended that man to be stopped from hitting the woman and held to the tree until he had plenty of time to think. They'll loosen and fall off in a couple of hours, and it didn't hurt him a bit."

"But I have a question. When I used the silver strands to stop the woman with the darkness in her middle, she did dissolve. Was I doing harm?" "Good question, gal. You did no harm because that was not a woman. It was an energy essence which formed a human-appearing body so it could move more freely among People. There are many of them on the planet right now as the darkness struggles to stay in control. One of the reasons the great darkness considers you to be so dangerous is that you can see the truth about these forms. It sounds like you also have what it takes to interrupt the pattern and send them back to their creators."

"It's so confusing," said Beauty. "I'm trying to remember everything, but sometimes there are strange contradictions. I have been taught more than once that there is no evil, only an imbalance, and I must do no harm.

So, if there is no evil, who would create those dangerous, dark forms and why would they do that?"

"Those trapped in darkness cannot see the light, only darkness. They live in fear and project that fear as blame onto everyone, even those trapped with them. They are trying to control their experience so they can feel safe, and that drive for safety is behind every act of greed, cruelty and aggression. Just as you create forms of light such as the silver threads, they can create forms of darkness. Right now those forms are in conflict with each other. It will take those who understand the importance of both to bring them back into the dance of life." Beauty grew very quiet. Gene recognized she had turned inward to her own soul and left her sitting in the garden. For a moment he thought he caught a glimpse of a Grizzly bending over her.

She returned to the porch in time for dinner, looking confident and peaceful. She searched the faces in front of her, and began speaking with a soft smile. "When I first told you my story a few days ago, I was filled with fear and anger. The terror of my meetings with darkness, the anger at the years of rejection and loneliness, anger at the hopelessness I felt. The fear you might ridicule me as others have made me so angry I almost bolted right then. I'm glad I didn't. Everything looks different now. The fear and anger are gone, although I understand the need for caution and strength while the forces of light and dark remain out of balance. But that caution and strength must come from a heart which only knows compassion for those caught on either side. Without compassion we will not be able to disarm those who grip the power of darkness, and we won't be able to awaken those who believe only the light should survive. It's clear now that the difficulties of my life were chosen to bring me to this moment and this understanding. I am ready to do whatever is mine to do. I am willing."

Gene wiped the corners of his eyes. Ariel was beaming. "Then tomorrow we travel," she said. "Beauty, you have traveled deep into the nurturing realms of darkness and brought back great secrets. Your wisdom will guide us. Eat well everyone, and rest soundly. We are about to get very busy."

In the morning they stepped outside at sunrise. "Traveler is completing another mission. The three of us will go together to our agreed meeting place and wait for him. Beauty, is there someone you would like to call to your side?" Beauty jumped with excitement. "Oh, yes! The wolf, and my three friends, Comfort and Shadow and Helper. Then there's the shining one and the great bear, and Margie. And the spider, and Mother," she finished with a whisper. "Hold it, just one for right now please. We don't want to disrupt the entire force field of life," said Ariel. Beauty thought only a moment. "Then it must be the wolf. We have a promise to keep, helping each other discover our purpose and our true names."

"You have already done that for her, although we'll let her tell you all about it. She knows our meeting place and is hoping to hear from you. Would you like to call her and tell her we're on our way? Her name is Sasha, Protector of Humans." Beauty's heart leaped and her understanding rearranged itself in a new pattern. The joy, the dragonfly, the feelings of confidence and peace and strength. These all came from Sasha! Throwing her arms wide and dropping all defenses, she poured her soul into her call. "SASHA! SASHA, I'm coming."

Reunion

Both light and shadow are the dance of Love. Love has no cause; it is the astrolabe of God's secrets. Lover and Loving are inseparable and timeless.

Rumi

Traveler and Sasha were flying back to Teacher. "You have mapped enough. Come back to me and we move to the next part of the plan." They heard the message at the same time and gladly left the grueling job of seeking and mapping and hiding. Extending their senses, they both immediately knew where to find him. He was pointing them toward the cave of dancing.

When the 'Call' came, Sasha sat bolt upright and fell off Traveler's back for the first time ever. As promised, Traveler swooped down and caught her, but was fierce in his scolding. "Clumsy fool, we are supposed to remain undetected and falling off is no way to do that. Besides, you startled me so I almost didn't catch you. Don't ever do that again!" But Sasha hardly heard her. "Traveler, she's coming, she called me. She even knows my true name. She is with Gene and Ariel, and they will meet us at the cave. She's back! I can feel her. I can touch her." Traveler, now caught up in Sasha's excitement, beat his powerful wings and flew faster toward the cave. Neither of them gave a thought to detection by the darkness.

Sasha and Traveler were the first to arrive. They looked to make sure there was plenty of wood, then gratefully settled in for a nap. It had been a long trip and they were anxious to hear what Teacher had to say was coming next. They didn't talk about the approach of Sasha's friend, as though it were too good to be true.

They were awakened as Star burst through the opening. The cub was almost fully grown but excitable as ever. He leaped on Sasha and they rolled and played, greeting each other both with wolf-like roughness and the language of the heart. There was a depth to the awareness in Star's eyes that was unmistakable. In the months Sasha and Traveler had been mapping, Star had been learning from Teacher and Messenger and serving as an assistant to both of them.

Many different children of the earth had come to learn and join in the coming effort. Most of them had been sent back to their homes, the locations carefully plotted on the planetary grid that Traveler and Sasha had been creating. They were instructed to wait for the call when all the light workers would be gathered for a great effort to bring the earth back in balance.

There was a stir in the air and the smell of tobacco smoke as Teacher stepped into the cave. "How is the wood supply?" were his first words. "We will dance tonight." Sasha leaped up at those words. "Does that mean she's coming?" "She is down the hill at the river. If you walk down there you can meet her and guide her to our cave." Sasha bounded out the entrance, Teacher yelling after him. "Pull in your energy. Stay hidden. We are only shielded in the cave, not out in the open." Sasha realized she could put everyone in danger. She stopped, pulled back into herself, and kept to the edges of rocks and bushes.

~~~~~~~~~~~~~~~~

Beauty and Ariel and Gene had traveled cautiously, disturbing the energy patterns of places as little as possible. Whenever they passed through sacred sites, which had natural shields, Beauty would practice ways to refine and strengthen her use of the silver threads. The shimmering ball of energy used to come only from her center, but she had learned to expand it so that it filled her. Now she could just lift her hand and a streak of silver would fly from her fingers. One day as they traveled, she was thinking about the many dimensions of music; how it was possible to hear it and also see its colors and inhale its scent. She had never forgotten its power to move her, and now a new dimension of possibility dawned in her mind. "Ariel," she asked, "do you think I could learn to send the threads just by speaking, or even by singing?" "You can learn to do anything you can imagine," was the encouraging reply.

Beauty thought about that for a long time, then came to Ariel again. "This power of the shining strands is much greater than I thought. If it is important to do no harm, then I believe the power must be guided by the wisdom of the heart. The mind is already engaged because you have to decide in order to use it, but that's not enough. My mind hasn't always made wise choices, particularly when my heart was closed. The heart must be in charge."

Ariel smiled gently. "Once again my dear, you have spoken aloud your purpose. Do you recognize it yet?" Beauty looked puzzled. "Living from the heart? Being heart centered? Heart minded?" Ariel shook her head. "One word is all you need." Beauty brightened. "Oh, well then, it must be love." "No, not quite love," said Ariel.
~~~~~~~~~~~~~~~~

Beauty stamped in frustration. "Then won't you just tell me? Obviously you know and I'm stuck with all this guessing."

"I can't do that," insisted Ariel. "You must awaken to it on your own. If you don't long for it enough to discover it on your own, you won't value it, just as you don't value it now because you don't notice it. Here is a hint. It was pointed out to you very early in your life by one you trusted. You have used it often over the years, on your own behalf and to help others. When you were unconscious and disconnected, it was still strong enough to keep you going. When you are living from your essence, it is the source of your deepest insights."

Beauty got very quiet, as she did often these days. Ariel held her breath. "My friend the spider told me".......... "Yes!" shouted Ariel. "Spider told me to use my wisdom." The shout exploded. "YES, YES, YES!" The two women threw their arms around each other and danced in a wild circle. Just then Gene returned from a search for food and joined them in the crazy dance when they breathlessly blurted out Beauty's remembrance. Finally they dropped to the ground in exhaustion. In a while a small fire was lit and food prepared. They appreciated the extravagance of being able to safely use fire without detection since they were in a sacred grove. As they settled in for the night, Ariel gave Beauty some instructions. "Before you sleep, go into the Silence and bring back as many memories as you can of using wisdom during your life. Those memories will help you focus it more sharply now."

Mostly Beauty remembered using her wisdom to not fully reveal herself to those who wouldn't understand. It was a wistful memory, tinged with sad loneliness. Then there was her spider friend; the memory of their conversations one of the bright spots in her life. She recognized that allowing her heart to choose made it possible to befriend Sasha, and closing her heart led to years of difficult relationships. Once she made the choice in her dream to feed the bear, her life had gotten better every day since. The memories all rushed in, weaving together like a fine tapestry, until she accepted fully that Wisdom was hers. It was the purpose she and Mother had selected for this Spirit Journey. In the morning she awoke first and slipped into her Silence, suddenly knowing they were near their destination. They would arrive before nightfall.

They traveled that day through increasingly barren country, and were grateful when they came upon a river in a steep valley; a river lined with trees and bushes. All three of them 'felt' the area cautiously, finding only neutral energy. Beauty's palm began to prickle, and she looked at the half moon mark that she had never given much attention. It was raised, as though it were scar tissue. Silver fire surged from her palm just as the bushes parted to reveal a beautiful wolf. They stared at each other, so used to meeting in the spirit world of dreams that it took a bit to realize this was the world of flesh and they could actually touch. Beauty stepped forward and laid her hand on Sasha's neck. They both gasped as they suddenly realized the depth of their connection. It was beyond the world of flesh and beyond the world of dreams. This was not a meeting. It was a reunion of souls. They sat together on the bank of the river, leaning on each other as they both slipped into the silence of communion. Ariel and Gene watched, stunned for a few moments, then turned and walked up the hill to give the two privacy.

Initiation

Ideas are catching, and no man can live where true ideas of wholeness and abundance and peace are being held without becoming more or less infected with them.

Charles Fillmore

It was nearing sunset when the entranced pair walked up the hill together. A curl of smoke was sending a welcoming signal from an opening at the top. As they entered the cave, the only two Beauty didn't know were introduced. Teacher welcomed her warmly, wiping a small tear from the corner of one eye. Messenger spread his wings wide and bowed. "I had the pleasure of watching you many times as you sat in nature choosing to open your heart again. Must say, I eavesdropped a bit. I hope you don't mind. It was my job to let everyone else know when you started waking up." Beauty laughed, and returned his bow. "I saw you once." Messenger winced. "Careless of me. No harm done though it seems." Ariel put an affectionate arm around her shoulder. "Do you know why we're here?" "For my name?" guessed Beauty. "Yes, my dear, it's time."

The figures on the wall flickered faintly in the fire-light; the red and black humans and animals, the white moon and stars, the yellow sun and growing corn. A faint memory of another ceremony stirred in Beauty, and her palm again tingled. Sasha's naming! It hadn't been a dream, she had been here! The return of another memory only linked the two of them more closely.

Once again the ancient ceremony began with Teacher's soft drumming and Traveler leading the dance. They all entered Dream Time and lost all sense of time. The slow dance around the fire began to pick up speed as the figures left the wall and joined them, notes of the flute weaving them together in story telling patterns. All were there, humans and four leggeds, wings and fins, and those with none of these. The dancers carried the memory of light and dark losing stability, creating a world of struggle and warfare. Waters were poisoned, smoke choked the air, food became scarce and many of the children of the earth forgot they were all related. Their dancing told of heroic acts restoring the sacred balance, returning the earth to its lush, green nature.

But many were lost in that struggle. Those who worked for light, in their self-righteousness, used their power to harm anyone they suspected of alliances with the other side. Those who worked for darkness were only concerned with how much power and how many resources they could command. Both did harmful things to each other. But, most of the children of the earth knew nothing about the forces of light and darkness, and were oblivious to anything but their own suffering. They were the ones most often harmed.

Then one came whose hands brought a healing balm. The shouts and demands of the light workers and the dark servants faded before a touch that closed wounds, straightened spines, and turned dead rivers into sparkling blue waters. The parched ground, long scorched by the fires of warfare and the blasts of white-hot light were touched by a fresh, clean rain and the corn began to grow again. The children of the earth turned away from the light workers and from the servants of dark and began to learn the ways of the healer. Kindness and respect were offered to everyone, no matter their former loyalties. Understanding of the gifts of both light and dark was reborn, and the world came back into balance.

The dance came to a joyful end, with much leaping and shouting. Power surged through all of them, reverberating on the walls of the cave with a low hum. A path cleared through the dancers and the white haired ancient one and Beauty stood looking at each other. She instantly spotted the great orb weaver on the old man's shoulder. "Spider, is that really you? Are you my spider friend from so long ago?" "Yes, it's true little one," replied the orb weaver. "But I can't really call you little one any more. Your wisdom has grown and your spirit is no longer small on the earth. I promised to be at your naming ceremony and we have waited a long time for you. So, let's begin." "But wait, will you tell me your name now?" cried Beauty. "My name is Weaver. I weave the stories of all the children of the earth into a web of life that supports them all. Tonight we weave your story into the web."

Weaver threw a silver strand to the cave ceiling and it told the story of a little girl who had been respectful and wise enough to do no harm to a great spider web. It told of how she had the wisdom to learn from one who was unlike herself, and use that wisdom well. More story tellers came forward and each story was caught by Weaver and woven into the pattern. The water moccasin told of its nest being honored, Gene spoke of the violent man being tied, Sasha of a young girl trusting a wolf. The great bear came forward. "She could have killed me, but she chose to feed me." Ariel spoke of Beauty's understanding that all power must be guided by the heart. The great spider wove and wove, and the ceiling was covered with shimmering lines of light. When the speakers had all finished, the ancient one bathed her in waves of sweet grass smoke, then fed her spirit with his rattling gourd. His raspy voice, rattling like dry leaves, finally spoke.

"You have come to wisdom and made it yours, choosing to live your purpose. Let your wisdom guide all who work to return balance and let your name be Sophia. Your lonely path is over. Now you walk with many companions." Spinning around the fire, his white hair flying and red blanket flapping, he cried, "Let us dance Sophia!" and the celebration began. They danced far into the night, tireless and joyful. The pounding of their feet on the cave floor sent a rhythmic message through the rocks and around the earth; "All is well." Many of the children of the earth, followers of both light and dark, slept better that night, not knowing why.

As the sounds of drum and flute finally came to an end, the ancient figures slowly returned to the walls. The great spider dropped to Sophia's shoulder for a moment before leaving. "You know my name now," she whispered. "You can call Weaver to your side any time you need me." Then Weaver swung on one of her own silver strands to catch the ancient one and landed on his shoulder just before he melted back into the cave wall. The fire was fed once more and those who remained were soon asleep. Sophia curled up in a blanket with Sasha's head resting on her hands.

They woke up hungry and realized no one had thought to bring food. Traveler said, "Hold on, I'll be right back. Gene, hop on. Let's go get breakfast." Remembering the size of the goose standing over him not long ago, Gene didn't argue but he did shudder as he mounted Traveler. Great wings lifted them in the air, Traveler 'turned' and they were gone.

Sasha, Star and Messenger went hunting. Sophia and Teacher and Ariel walked down to the river for water, arriving just as Traveler and Gene popped back into view laden with provisions from Ariel's house. Traveler dove for a reedy bank full of his favorite food and the humans downed a large meal of bread and cheese and sausages and fruit. No one objected to having a nap in the sun. They returned to the cave after a mid-afternoon swim. Traveler helped carry more wood and the remaining food up the hill.

Teacher and Gene and Ariel were deep in conversation as the others stacked supplies and shook out blankets. Sasha and Sophia walked back into the sunlight together, sharing the details of their separate adventures as they sat on the warm, mica flecked rock. Sophia's eyes sparkled with an idea. "Weaver said I could call her any time I need her now that I have my name. You haven't met my kid friends yet. I want to call them and see if they will come." Shivering with hope and dread, she let her full voice call out. Shadow and Comfort and Helper grew out of three glinting pieces of mica and the old friends jumped on each other, laughing and patting and swinging each other around.

"You still look like kids," exclaimed Sophia. "Good plan isn't it?" was the response from Helper. "That way you will always recognize us but those who don't know us won't think we amount to much. Being a kid is a great disguise." Sophia instantly saw the wisdom and laughed. She turned to introduce Sasha, but Shadow piped in. "Oh, we already know her. We watched many of the times you two met in dream time. Ariel told us to make sure you wouldn't miss each other. It was quite a tough job sometimes, especially when you decided to go hiding." "Well she doesn't know you," insisted Sophia after checking with Sasha. "Sasha, these three clowns were my first friends. We had great fun together, and I was never lonely when Comfort and Shadow and Helper came around." She thought a minute then turned to the kids again. "You three disappeared long before I closed my heart. Where did you go? Why didn't you answer when I called?"

"That was really hard", answered Comfort. "Ariel told us you would have to walk alone for a long time in order to learn enough to come into your wisdom. We were always there watching, but we couldn't help you. A couple of times we almost broke the silence, and Ariel was really angry. I promise, you do not want that lion/lady annoyed at you. She's terrifying and she has a temper."

Sophia thought of the bitterly lonely years, pain dropping on her heart like acid, and knew those years had forged a steel in her that would never allow the light to be used for harm. Wisdom had carried a great cost, but she had no regrets. Shaking off the past, she uttered a challenge.

"When's the last time any of you rode a rainbow? Let's do it. Come on Sasha, we'll show you how." All five jumped and slid across the sky on a great bow of light, hair flying, Sasha with her mouth open and tongue hanging out. They whooped and howled with delight as they played. Anyone looking on only would have seen a mist suddenly arise and five beams of sunlight. Anyone except Ariel of course. She stepped out of the cave and recognized instantly that Sophia and Sasha had begun their dance in earnest. They had much to teach each other.

The woman and the wolf left the cave on the hill and traveled east, carrying provisions for a few days for Sophia and knowledge of where to find food and shelter along the way. When the landscape changed and the friends stepped into a deep forest, both of them felt they had come home. They walked for long periods in comfortable quiet, feeling little need for conversation. Sasha tried to teach Sophia how to extend her essence to 'find' but the woman wasn't catching on. Both of them could easily slip into Silence and sense the life all about them and both of them could communicate easily with those who understood the language of the heart, but there the similarity ended.

Many of those who had been trained by Teacher were back in their own homes, knowing visitors might arrive at any time, and Sasha carried the locations easily in her memory. One of their first stops was at a small house in a clearing. Sasha remembered it as the house of the lost boy. The People with the gun was not there. Instead a teenage boy stepped outside to meet them. "Hi, my name is Matt. Teacher told me you would be coming. Let me get my pack and I'll come with you. We need to leave before dad gets back. He hasn't changed his opinion of wolves at all."

Sasha thought it strange the boy had grown so much, but remembered what Ariel kept saying about time not being linear. "So, Matt," asked Sasha, "Do you know your purpose? Do you know your true name yet?" "The one I was born with," replied the boy. "Matthew means gift of the spirit, and it is my purpose to sense the approach and the intentions of spirits. That's why I wasn't afraid of you and Traveler when you found me by the rock and led me home. Speaking of sensing, have you noticed you're being followed?"

Sophia blinked in surprise and Sasha spun around but couldn't see anyone. "I know you're there young wolf, so come on out," called Matt. Head low, Star stepped from behind a bush, expecting a scolding as usual. "Come on, you can join us," said Sasha. "I can't teach Sophia how to 'find', so maybe I'll try with you. Did you tell anyone you were leaving? Does Teacher know you followed us?" Star looked glum. “No. I was afraid I wouldn’t be allowed.” “Then you should go back. Do you know the way?” “No.”

Sophia was grinning. Her friend sounded just like a mother. “Matt, can you get a message back to Teacher?” she asked. “We have a communication network but we’re only supposed to use it for something important,” he answered. Sophia nodded. “This is important. We don’t want them wasting a lot of time looking for this pup. They have enough to do. Just send word that Star is with us.” They stopped in the barn and Matt tied a note to the leg of a pigeon and set it free. They left the clearing together, moving back into the shelter of the forest.

They traveled almost randomly, heading in no particular direction but seeking always to find those who were waiting for them. They would come to a town or a farm in Sasha’s memory to find any number of the children of the earth waiting for them; sometimes just one or two and sometimes dozens. If all of these were to help bring the earth back into balance, they must learn the language of the heart and the sound of silence. Most of them had learned some of it from Teacher, but they needed to know how it applied to their individual purpose and how to use their own spirit power with wisdom and an open heart. Sasha and Sophia had mastered their life purpose so well that they made wonderful teachers, but they remained cautious about how much to share and when.

The companions found themselves camping in the forest one night, several people from the last town traveling with them. Sophia had been teaching them how to gather their personal spirit energy and direct it through their fingers, and they wanted to stay with her and sharpen their skills. One person thought the whole thing nonsense but would not let his wife travel an unknown distance and direction without him. Pete had a good heart but a closed mind and wouldn’t even attempt the exercises. They settled around the campfire after dinner and the lessons continued. Sophia lifted her hand and five beams of light shined forth. "Pass it around the circle and send an intention for steadiness and strength to each other." They did, and the light made it all the way around. Pete sat off to one side, shaking his head. "I don't know what all of you are doing but nothing is happening. Big waste of time going on here and we should all just go home," was his comment.

Matt, who was learning very quickly hunched down next to him, hands held out. "Pete, let your fingers just touch mine." Pete did, looking sour. "Now, move them apart just a little, and watch for light." Pete jumped, surprised. "OK, I saw some light but what good is it?" Just then a ball of darkness rolled across the forest floor, pausing near each one of them and headed for Pete. "Matt, stay connected," cried Sophia. "Everyone else send your energy to Matt, quickly. Matt, send it into one of Pete's hands. Pete, use your other hand to touch the ball of dark." Eyes popping, Pete did as he was told and the ball dissolved. "What was that and what just happened?" he asked with a shaky voice. "It was an energy probe sent by the darkness," answered Matt. "I felt it coming but didn't know what to do." Sophia's answer sobered them all. "It was looking for us and would have carried back the energy pattern of each one of us to its makers. We must remain alert for them and dissolve every one we find."

Matt thought about that for a few minutes, sensing the spirit behind the dark balls, then said, "No, that's not right. They aren't messengers, they are beacons. Transmitters. We do have to dissolve all of them we can, but it's because they can become part of us and bring their makers to us by acting as a beacon. We need to check our own personal energy frequently to make certain we are not carrying one of them." Sophia shuddered at the thought of being found. They all went to sleep sobered, determined to learn as much as they could about their own spirit power.

They continued to move cautiously from village to town, checking often for the balls of darkness. In each place a few would join their group, some human and some not, and a few would stay behind to teach what they had learned to those who couldn't travel. The language of the heart was central to all their conversations, and words became less necessary and more meaningful. For those who learned how to touch the sound of silence, Sophia began teaching the use of silver strands whenever they stopped to rest or eat, and Sasha taught 'finding' by extending energy and absorbing the energy of every place into cell memory. The knowledge spread through the communities of the children of the earth like a growing spider web. An energy of excitement and urgency was growing and people began to ask when they would meet the dark forces. "Matt and Star, go find Teacher quickly. Tell him all you know and ask his advice. We don't know how far to go or how many more people to teach," Sophia said. "Then ask Traveler to bring you back quickly so you can continue to help. Go safely!"

The Call

I don't know what your destiny will be, but one thing I do know; the only ones among you who will be really happy are those who have sought and found how to serve.

Albert Schweitzer

The two began to name their teaching travels "The Call". They ran between hamlets and towns swiftly and tirelessly, Sophia's hand on Sasha's back giving her the speed and stamina of the wolf. Sasha's finding skills kept their direction true, and Sophia spun a web of silvery energy, masking their presence as they passed through towns and farms and empty stretches of country. They dared not fly or 'turn' in time or dimensions. The great darkness was alerted and watching closely for any sign of them. They paused to eat and sleep during the heat of the day. They sent out gentle probes and found allies trained by Teacher, waiting for them with food and shelter. They were carrying The Call for the Gathering of light workers, delivering messages at key points on the grid.

On the tenth day as they approached their shelter, they knew they were too tired to go on. Even the sense of urgency, of time running out, was not enough to keep them moving without more rest. Sasha found their next refuge, a small farm tucked in a valley. The house and barns were nearly hidden in a curve of a hill, thick with trees. As they entered, Sasha was panting and Sophia could no longer maintain the silvery web she was using to camouflage them. They were given water and a soft place to rest, and they both sank into the softness with trembling legs, and fell instantly asleep.

Sasha woke with a start, realizing she had not felt to test the hearts of those in this place. How could she be so careless, putting Sophia in danger and risking the success of their mission? She circled her sleeping friend protectively, probing lightly for clues about the intent of those who kept this place. She found nothing. No sense of human or animal; only the soft humming of the insect world and the whisper of life in the veins of plants.

She relaxed a bit as she realized if harm had been intended, it would have happened as they slept. Still, safety held the greatest importance, and Sophia was too tired to shield them with energy, so Sasha tried something she had never done before. With all her being, she sent out a call for Sophia's friend, Shadow. He came at once, materializing from a sun ray shining in the window and bringing Helper and Comfort with him. "Please help us", said Sasha. "We need a safe way to hide so we can get more rest. There is so little time left, and we are so tired."

Shadow, Helper and Comfort joined hands, surrounding the two exhausted runners. A soft buzzing noise began, slowing growing stronger. A light was passing through the three, making them look like they were glowing from the inside. Then Shadow said, "turn, now". All five of them winked out of the room, to another where/when. Sophia never stirred, so Sasha curled up next to her and went back to sleep.

They woke naturally and easily at the same time. "I feel so much better," said Sophia. "I wonder how long we've been asleep." "Three days", said a voice behind her, and Sophia whirled to see Shadow and his two companions, sitting on a window sill, watching them and grinning. "Oh no, we're going to be too late! We have failed", cried Sophia. Helper stepped forward and jumped into the conversation.

"We brought you to a different where/when so you could get enough rest to continue your mission. We'll take you back to exactly the right time. Nothing is lost. Even those who were keeping the farm house for your shelter haven't noticed you were gone. We'll take you back to just before they come in to bring you food, and they won't have a clue about us. We must remain a secret in case you need us again."

"Oh Helper, thank you so much," Sophia cried as she hugged him, then reached for the other two. "Thank you all, but how did you know to come?" "Sasha called us," was the reply. "You two have become so close, you speak as one heart. Your deep caring for each other is your greatest power. Remember that if it becomes difficult to fulfill your purpose." "And remember to call us if you need us," piped Comfort. "We're always just a time-slip away."

The three companions surrounded Sophia and Sasha again, and the buzzing sound and glowing light began to build. "Turn now", said Shadow. They were back in the farmhouse, watching as Helper, Shadow and Comfort slipped away on a sunbeam. The door opened and a woman came in, delighted to see them awake. "We have a feast prepared in the barn. It's the only place big enough for all of us to eat. Come with me and meet the other children of the earth who are waiting to see you. You haven't had very much time to rest, but we have some help for you."

Sophia put her hand on the back of Sasha's neck and they walked into the barn together to discover an amazing crowd of beings. Sophia dodged as Traveler greeted them first, landing on Sasha's back, pecking at her ears, flapping his wings and whooping with delight. Traveler jumped down and bowed as an ancient man in a red blanket stepped forward with greetings, followed by others anxious to get a glimpse of the famous pair.

The crowd finally settled down and gathered in a circle, conversation buzzing pleasantly as food was passed around. The ancient man stood and walked around the circle, shaking a small rattle in his hand. Messenger flew in the open barn door and landed on the old man's shoulder. "I come from Teacher with instructions", said the great bird. "The time has come for the children of the earth who remember the light to be ready to gather. Watch for a message by pigeon or eagle, then follow it and come quickly. Sophia and Sasha, continue your work for a little while longer, but be alert for the message to gather."

~~~~~~~~~~~~~~~~

For Sasha and Sophia, as they taught, their skills grew and expanded and became more closely shared. Occasionally they would slip away together and sit in deep communion in the great Silence. Much like riding rainbows with Shadow and Helper and Comfort, they would sometimes soar through galaxies. The beauty rocked their very cores, but there was so much of it that they learned to let it in and thrill in it without becoming attached. The lights glowing off great clouds, punctuated by diamond brilliance and lying on deep black velvet space was an experience of pure eternity. They remained individual enough to dance with delight, bouncing the
~~~~~~~~~~~~~~~~

grandeur between them like playful children, yet united enough to share every instant completely.

Once Sophia captured a moment in time and tossed it toward Sasha like a ball. "Here, catch!" Sasha leaped and easily snapped her jaws around it - and winked out like an extinguished candle. Sophia stood in shock, not knowing what to do. "Sasha, where are you? Sasha!" For a moment fear clamped her heart, then she remembered that "here" and "now" and "then" were all made up, so she wrapped all the love she could muster then flung it in every direction on gleaming silver threads. Her soul moved into "finding" and in a moment the two were reunited. But where were they? In a city. Quickly Sophia recognized it as the city where her house was, that she had just left – just a few dáys ago? A thousand years ago? She shook her head to clear the sense of disorientation.

Sasha looked at her quizzically. "You threw me a time bite and now here we are. What did you have in mind?" "Sorry, I wasn't exactly thinking," said Sophia. "But I'm sure it's not an accident. How about we make a round of my old haunts and see what pops up?" Sasha gave her a strange look. "Well, that's not exactly a plan, but lets keep as hidden as we can and give it a try. The darkness did find you here before, right?" Sophia shivered.

Staying hidden in a city with a wolf at your side was problematical, but Sasha had done it before with Traveler. They found a place to hide and waited until night to move, and then avoided lights. Sophia wanted to find her friend Margie so they went to her house. It was dark but unlocked so they slipped in carefully. They did not use the ability to send out their essence and sense, but just walked quietly from room to room. They found Margie in her office, the blue light of her computer screen flickering slightly; a dozen messages blinking on her answering machine. She was slumped in her chair, unmoving. Sophia stifled a gasp with her hand as she realized Margie was enveloped in a dark, fuzzy haze, her wide eyes begging Sasha's help.

Sasha's reply was instant. "Let's take her quickly to another moment in time. I'll catch one, you use your silver to cut her loose and bind her to you, and we'll make the jump. Quickly now." Sophia understood instantly. Trusting Sasha to handle the time bit, she sliced away the dark haze, bound the three of them together, and they winked away before the disturbance in the field was noticed.

They landed in their most recent camp before anyone had found them missing. Margie woke up startled and shaken, impressing them all with her vocabulary of swear words. She calmed down when she saw Sophia, then turned to the woods and vomited fiercely. "What the hell was that cold dark? I remember being held down. It wanted me to do something, find someone. I remember struggling and the bonds getting tighter. It was all fear and anger and hopelessness. I remember silver stuff cutting me loose, and I think part of me went with it. What? What?"

Sophia took her hands. "They were looking for me. You are my friend and they thought you could lead them to me. We have you now. The only parts you have lost are those that allowed them to trap your spirit, so you are truly free now. We will teach you the language of the heart if you like, so you can talk to all of us." "Honey, if that kind of blackness is hunting you, I'm not sure its such a good idea to be your friend or learn the language of your other friends," groaned Margie. Sophia patted her. "Get a good night's sleep. Morning will be sweet, I promise."

Food and hot tea and the softest blankets appeared and Margie slept. Sophia and Sasha curled around her, moved into the Silence and invited her spirit to join them.

Together they carried her through all their memories in this time. When she woke up, there was peace in her eyes and a set to her chin. "Well, we have work to do. You two better start teaching me now." "You're on," crowed Sophia as she hugged her friend. "We need you to gather the very best of the spiritual teachers you have been helping and bring them to join us. But first you have to know that time and distance and dimensions are something we just make up in this reality, and anything we make up can be shifted. You must learn to shift and dance and 'turn' in space and eternity if you want to help us." Sophia looked at Margie closely. "The best way I know to teach you all that is rainbow riding. Are you willing?" "What!!" gasped Margie. Sophia took her hand. "Do you trust me?" Margie looked a bit wobbly but she nodded.

"Shadow, Comfort, Helper, its play time. We have a new friend." The three popped in on a dust mote and surrounded Margie, instantly gaining her trust. Then all of them blinked away for a while to the sound of squeals of laughter. They came back, arms around each others shoulders to find Sasha waiting for them with Star. Star was assigned the task of teaching Margie the language of the heart, while Sasha and Sophia helped both of them learn the sound of silence.

As they traveled, Star became more and more adept at finding; so good that all he needed was a description of a place, or a heart shared memory of another in order to go directly there. He quickly learned to find people as well as places, and before long he could find feelings. Margie would share information about one of the teachers she knew, Star would pinpoint the time and place and Sasha or Traveler would shift time and dimensions to carry Margie to the teacher with an invitation to join the group. The first time Margie met Traveler she stared at the bird, then at Sophia, hands on hips. "I suppose this is the goose you said was stalking you." "Stalking was your word, not mine," shot back Sophia.

All the years of loneliness Sophia had endured were erased with these companions, and she blossomed, no longer afraid to use and fine tune all her gifts. But something was happening to Star. He had a growing feeling that something was missing; something very important. It was almost as though there was a leaking hole in him somewhere, but he looked just fine. When he asked his companions what was wrong with him, they couldn't find anything. "Star, you worry too much," said Sasha. "Every day you get stronger at finding, and we can all feel the goodness of your heart. You are fast and loyal and fun and we love you. There is nothing wrong with you." So Star stopped mentioning his fears, but it was strongest when he practiced the sound of silence.

Another Dimension

The real voyage of discovery consists of not in seeking new landscapes but in having new eyes.

Marcel Proust

The feeling of something missing grew stronger and more troubling. One night Star slipped away into the dark forest alone, seeking intently for help. The woods were deep and there were no sun warmed rocks, so he curled tightly around himself to stay warm. Gathering all his courage, he cleared his mind, slipped into the silence and listened with every cell. At first he just heard the whispers of insects and tree sap and an occasional small animal, but then a new sound began to grow. At first it was like the soft whisper of a breeze, but became stronger and stronger until Star found himself in a howling gale that picked him up flung him in a dizzying vortex of sound and motion.

He was suddenly dropped with a bump and, hackles upright on his back, found himself in the middle of a pack of wolves. They were not aggressive or threatening. They sniffed him curiously and one or two brushed a face against his or licked his ear, just as they would with a member of their pack. Star's fear melted and curiosity took its place. "Where am I? Who are you? What is this place?" he asked. Not only was there no answer, it was clear they didn't even hear his questions. They didn't have the language. Frustrated, Star slipped into finding. Of course it didn't work since he had no idea what to find. He wandered the packs territory, searching now for a way back, but the feeling of something missing got stronger and stronger and clouded his senses. Once he wandered into the cave of a she-wolf that seemed vaguely familiar. She recognized him, but warned him away, protecting her young.

The pack Star found himself in clearly had a leader. Sometimes he felt the urge to challenge him, to take the leadership away, but he quelled that urge. He didn't want leadership, not with this pack. He wanted to go home. He wanted to go back to his friends.

Star wandered a long time, finally entering the life of the pack half heartedly. They accepted him; all the while his loneliness grew. He could no longer imagine living without the language of the heart, and no one here had it. His body matured and grew powerful and the females began to send hints of invitation, but Star could only think of his lost companions. He often went into the woods alone, seeking the silence, and the vortex he hoped would take him back, but there was no sign of the wild energy of the vortex.

The Silence came to him naturally and easily, and it was much like he had learned in the other place. Star would find a warm place to curl up and let his breathing slow and his eyes slip into a softer focus. He could easily feel the comings and goings of animals and birds of many kinds, although none seemed to share his finely tuned sense. The hum of insect life, the light, sweet sound of sap moving through plants, the thrilling power of the trees and the barely perceptible thrum, thrum of rock life soothed him and gave him hope. Perhaps there wasn't that much difference here. Star decided to teach the people of this world the language of the heart and the sound of Silence.

He would make it a game and begin with the cubs, who were less cautious than the adults. He had already shared some playful tussling with them and won their trust, so he would just add another dimension.

He lured them into a circle with a favorite tug of war game, then laid flat and unmoving with his ears perked. Curious, they nudged him, batted his tail, nipped an ear, but Star remained motionless except for his eyes following them. He sent out the word "play," attached to the feeling of fun and adventure. After a while one cub stopped suddenly, shook its head, then leaped playfully on top of Star, who immediately jumped up and turned it into a game of "catch me if you can," then laid flat again only ears and eyes moving. Another cub caught on after a while, then another. By the next day, when Star sent out the word "play" they would all come running, ready for a romp.

The weeks went by swiftly then. Star taught them only words that carried feeling at first, like safe – hungry - caution. Then words that pointed to things, like water – rock - rabbit. The day he taught them "wolf," referring to self and "rabbit," referring to the little long ears, a breakthrough into abstract thought happened and the young ones begged to teach the rabbit as well. The adults began to notice a strange new feeling in their pack and it was good. Before long it was not unusual to see an adult head snap up as an idea was caught from Star or one of the young ones. It was here Star began teaching concepts. Love. Trust. Respect. He knew if he could teach them the sound of Silence next, they would learn to feel all life as one, just as he had learned in that other world.

~~~~~~~~~~~~~~~~

Margie caught up with Sophia when Traveler brought her back from her latest trip to find teachers. "Where is
~~~~~~~~~~~~~~~~

Star?" she asked. "You know how he wanders off sometimes. He's been gone too long though. I haven't seen him in a couple of days," was the answer. Concerned, they searched and called. Sasha helped, using her strongest finding skills and traveling to the times and places she knew Star had been with them. It was as though Star had never existed. There was no trace of his essence anywhere. When Sasha arrived at the spot where Star had first been found, he recognized the feeling. Wherever Star had come from, he was gone, and Sasha was not able to cross the barrier between worlds.

"I'm sorry Sophia", Sasha said. "I can't help you find Star. I've searched and searched, and I find no trace of him. I don't know what we're going to do to find him." At that Sophia had a thought. "What if we…what if we find Teacher? I'll ask him to help us enter the dream time. Maybe there we can find him." "Not us, Sophia, you. You must do this one without me. I'd only be in your way. I will stay here and continue our work."

Sophia quickly found Traveler. "Please, dear friend, take me to Teacher as fast as you can. We'll have to risk 'turning' in time. There's not a moment to waste." Traveler spread his wings and the two blinked out of sight as soon as Sophia landed on his back. They flew together, not under a sunny sky or bright starlight, but in a dense fog. "Traveler where are we? How can you see where you're going?" pleaded Sophia. Traveler explained. "I've learned some new things from Ariel and her owls. Our intention is to skip across time and find Teacher, and to remain hidden and keep him hidden. The fog hides us, and our intention delivers us safely to our destination".

As he finished speaking, they landed in front of a cave opening and Teacher called them from inside. "Come on in. The fire is ready, so let's not waste any time. We will dance into dream time." Sophia walked in and looked around the inside of the cave. It was different from the last cave they had met in. There were few petro glyphs on the walls. Just a small band of wolves, a splash of stars in white, and an eagle feather.

As before, Traveler began the dance, raising and lowering his wings and moving slowly around the fire. An orb weaver spider lowered itself from the ceiling and hung above them on a silken strand, waiting. Teacher began drumming softly and Sophia felt her eyes go out of focus. She gathered her memories and feelings and impressions about the young cub, and put all her attention on her image of Star, holding the image in her heart with tenderness and love. The love radiated outward from her in great, golden waves. It was a glowing nimbus reaching far beyond the confines of the cave, past space and time. She felt a strong wind take her, then she was whirled in a golden vortex, never noticing the silver strand tangled in one strand of her hair. She kept her attention tightly locked on Star and let the ride take her to the edge of a forest.

Sophia knew instantly she was far from familiar territory. She couldn't get her bearings or find a sense of anywhere or anywhen that she knew. Just as she had with her cat Bones, she called and called to Star with her heart in her voice. A wolf walked up next to her and nuzzled her hand. Shaken, she asked, "Who are you?" To her great relief, he answered in the language of the heart. "Sophia, it's Star. Don't you know me?" "My friend Star is a young wolf cub," she replied. "You are a grown wolf. You can't be Star." "But Sophia, I've been here for many seasons. A whole pack of wolf cubs has grown up since I got here. And I think you'll be pleased. I've taught them our language, and the Silence."

"But in my time," argued Sophia, "you've only been gone a few days. Where are we? When are we?" Star answered with a wolfish shrug and a shake of his head.

"I've missed you all so much. I taught all the young wolves here so I wouldn't forget, and now they are teaching other children of this forest. I want so much to go back with you to Sasha and all our friends. I tried to 'find' my way back many times but there is no trail to follow."
"Then lets try together," said Sophia. "If we both focus as one, maybe 'finding' will work."

So they filled their minds with images and memories of Sasha, sending their essence out together for even the faintest wisp of a direction. When that failed, they tried Teacher. They thought hard about him, the things he taught them, how he walked, his pipe, and everything else they could remember, and sent those memories out in every direction as they extended their essence. Nothing. Sophia's reddish brown hair was glinting in the sunlight, and Star noticed something. "Sophia, are you starting to get gray hair? There's something silver attached to one of your curls." Sophia carefully brushed her hand over the area Star indicated, and came away with a silver thread. With a thrill, she realized it was a strand of spider web.

"Star!" she squealed with excitement. "This is it; this is our way home. Spider sent this to help us. We must be very careful not to harm it." Sophia bound Star to herself using some of her own silver strands, then carefully wrapped the end of hers and the spiders' together. "Be very still," she instructed Star. "Don't jerk or fall or do anything sudden. We must both trust for this to get us back home." Then she very gently moved her body to start a small wave in the web strand, sending her intention and love along with it. Without dropping Sophia's silver strand, the web strand whipped into the air then spun the two of them around and around until they were caught in a ball. With a sharp jerk, they were whipped past a blinding array of stars and sunbeams, and landed with a thump in the middle of the cave.

Teacher and Traveler and the great spider were waiting for them. "It is time, the orb weaver said, to dance Star's true name," and she wove a web around the top of the cave, each strand telling a story of Star's life. She finished by saying, "Star has brought the light of knowledge and wisdom to a new dimension. He is a true member of the wolf clan, a teacher of distinction. Let him be known as Star, the Light Bringer." Teacher was already drumming with all his heart, and the small group danced and danced around the fire, in celebration of Star.

When they had finished dancing, all panting with delight, Teacher announced, "I am going back with you, and the great spider comes with me. The children of the light and the children of the dark are about to meet. We must bring the dark and light into balance or this world will end." Teacher touched the eagle feather and Messenger swooped into the room. Teacher held a picture of a particular valley firmly in his attention, instructing his companions to enter the Silence with him and become familiar with it so they could find it and lead others there. "Messenger, tell all the eagles and pigeons to gather the children of the earth who have been trained and bring them to this valley as quickly as possible. It is time."

Final Conflict

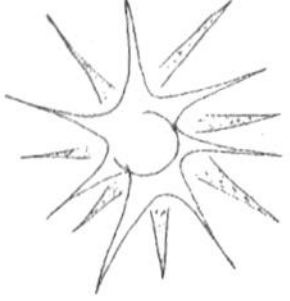

Where there is great love, there are always miracles.

Willa Cather

On a misty morning Sophia and Sasha's companions walked out of the forest all at once, coming fully visible before they realized the broad meadow in front of them was filled with the children of dark. An electric shock passed between the two armies, and before anyone could think or speak, a great roar went up and they rushed toward each other, closing the distance in a few heartbeats. Sophia cried "No!! It's too soon, wait, wait," but no one heard or paused. In moments children of the light and the dark were falling, some blinking out of visibility. Sophia leapt into the middle, separating the fighters with the force of her hands.

Sasha's howl of anguish rent the air as people on both sides were overcome. The howl cracked something open in Sophia's heart. "This is wrong! Harm is wrong!" She grieved as deeply for the dark ones as for the children of light. She began using the silver threads to pull fallen dark ones away as Sasha came to the aid of the light beings. The battle quickly lost steam as so many fell. Sasha and Sophia worked frantically to heal and separate the forces. As the dark ones withdrew to the far side of the clearing,

Sophia led her friends back into the forest and called for Shadow. "Shadow we need you desperately. Come hide us!" called Sophia with all her strength.

Shadow, Helper and Comfort unwound from a tree trunk, bringing a friend. "This job's too big for us. The dark ones are already finding their courage and coming to look for you. We brought help," said Shadow. A great, tawny lion seemed to arise from the ground, then stood and stretched into the magnificent feminine form of Ariel. She waved her arm and wraith-like owl shapes began to circle the group, enclosing them in a heavy fog. To the other army, nothing was visible but the slightly misty forest. They stayed hidden for another day, hoping the call had gone out and all the people and other beings they had been teaching would arrive in time.

And they did arrive, led by eagles and pigeons, coming in groups of five and ten and fifty into the fog of the owls. Ariel taught the newcomers as quickly as she could about the illusion of time and how to use it effectively by keeping their personal energy field clean, intending only the best for every living being. As the following morning dawned, they all knew it was time. The fog lifted as Ariel called her owls and moved to a high hill.

Ariel directed owl wraiths from the hill with waves of her arms, confusing the aggressive and protecting the fallen. Teacher drummed and the eagles and pigeons arose, followed by the children of the earth they had brought from all over the land. Teacher drummed, and the ancient one wearing a red blanket led his dancers into the fray, white hair flying as he whirled. Orb Weaver picked off combatants one by one, tying them safely out of the way.

She stood at the precipice, arms outstretched, the lavender rose in her right hand. Sasha was at her side, repelling all beings who dared the precipice to stop Sophia. The field of battle was a struggle of mind and intention, help and harm, love and terror flying everywhere. Great silver threads poured from her center in all directions, shielding her companions and hissing with steam when they hit the darkness. Silver streamed from her fingers and her eyes, and her voice rose in a song that carried the power of pulsing stars.

The Light Healers rushed to the side of everyone who fell, dark or light, and helped them to where they could best heal or transform. The command, "do no harm" reverberated in their hearts. When some began to arise from the dark forces to help with the fallen, there was a shimmer in the field of battle. Something had shifted. Sophia sent the dark ones some of her silver threads, offering protection and assistance. One of the first to accept the help was a great, black form, immensely powerful. For a moment it appeared to contemplate the possibility of having a new weapon. Then it cradled half a dozen of the wounded, closing over them with deep dark, and used the silver thread to bind wounds.

Unaware of the help pouring into her from Weaver and her other friends, she gave her all, the silver threads becoming indistinguishable from her now glowing body. Dark and light stood in sharp contrast all over the valley. They no longer fought, but rather danced together in a rhythm not unlike a heartbeat. Here and there a being not able to balance blinked out of sight.

As the rhythm intensified, Sophia pealed an exultant scream, knowing it was finished. For one brief moment she looked at Sasha, her eyes beaming love. Joy shot through her, instantly passing through the silver threads to her friends, then to everyone else. The hot, silver fire she had become blinked out of sight with a giggle that rang across the fields.

Sasha felt her leave. It was both a moment of celebration and a blow to the heart. She fell to her knees, aching, laughing and crying all at once. Star was at Sasha's side. "We will teach Sophia's story to the children of the earth. As long as we live, we will teach them how to honor both the dark, where gestation and healing happens, and the light, where learning and growth happen. We will teach them balance so they will do no harm from now on."

"And one day, we will be with her again," whispered Sasha.

Epilogue

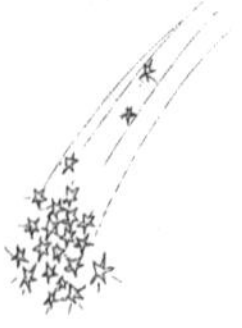

The most powerful weapon on earth is the human soul on fire.

Ferdinand Foch

The Star cluster pulsed with life and power. In this massive dance of energy, size had no meaning and time did not exist. Stardust and red giants danced together, whirling in the eternal moment. Colors sparkled in the brilliant light and sound wove ideas into molecules. Sophia reached out with her awareness and, like long, curling hair floating in the sea, tendrils wisped to everywhen. Her little girl giggle rollicked into a physical reality, and a new game began. One tendril touched pain and she instantly followed it to a place where the duality of suffering and joy were locked in a struggle. Sasha was already there, waiting for her. They could feel Mother smiling as they agreed to go again. Perhaps this time they would be able to remember Mother.

Postlude

Every child comes with the message that God is not yet discouraged of man.

Rabindranath Tagore

"Nanna," whispered her great grandson. "What were the golden waves of light that kept showing up? I could hear them playing music!" "That was the energy of love, little one," great grandmother replied. "Love crosses all boundaries of time and space. It goes everywhere and everywhen."